Prais‹

"These are unique, fresh, twisted, intelligent stories."

Daniel P. Calvisi
Author of *Story Maps: How to Write a GREAT Screenplay*

"This author has the same delicious darkness [as Stephen King], but with an additional touch of a strange wit and humor... How can something so dark be so addicting?"

Jennifer Elizabeth Hyndman
Author/Blogger of *Angels in the Underworld*

"The voices are well created, the story lines are interesting, and Hatton has a good touch as to when to make things explicit and when to leave them below the surface."

David S. Atkinson
Author of *Apocalypse All the Time*

Praise for *Dead Size*

"*Dead Size* by Sawney Hatton is a fantastic blend of detective story, dark comedy, and waking daydream—a surrealist painting of a novel."

Eirik Gumeny
Author of *Exponential Apocalypse*

"The novel showcases Hatton's powerful blend of quirky humor and spot-on characterization... builds to a wild and unpredictable conclusion."

James Chambers
Author of *The Engines of Sacrifice*

Praise for *Uglyville*

"Unconventional in the best of ways. I found myself surprised, disturbed, and turning pages."

Daniel Braum
Author of *The Night Marchers and Other Strange Tales*

If you enjoy this book, please support the author by posting a review on Amazon, Goodreads, your personal blog, and/or social media pages.

Thanks for reading.

Everyone Is a Moon

WRITTEN STUFF BY SAWNEY HATTON

Dead Size (A Dark Comedy Novel)
Uglyville (A Noir Novella)
Everyone Is a Moon (A Dark Fiction Collection)
The Devil's Delinquents (An Occult Novella)
Dirty Spirits (A Paranormal Novel)

EDITED STUFF BY SAWNEY HATTON

What Has Two Heads, Ten Eyes, and
Terrifying Table Manners?
(A Sci-Fi/Horror Anthology)

EVERYONE
IS A MOON

strange stories by
Sawney Hatton

Cover design by
Fredrick Richard

Artwork in "The Dark at the Deep End"
by Patrick McGuiverstein

Published by Dark Park Publishing
First Print Edition: September 2018
ISBN: 978-0-9886444-9-6

To everybody who
believed in my words.

CONTENTS

Some Graphic Material Herein.
Reader Discretion Advised.

PREFACE

My memories of my childhood are hazy at best. More often they are blank spots, locked rooms for which I no longer have the key.

And yet, I do vividly remember snippets and snapshots of certain moments. My father holding me while we peered down the length of the derailed Florida-bound train we'd been riding on. Screaming for my mother while the nurses wheeled me away from her on my way to get a tonsillectomy. Shrinking away from my dying grandfather in his hospice room because I feared he would make me sick too. A railroad safety slide show shown in my elementary school featuring graphic photos of bloody faces and mangled flesh. The decaying carcass of a Dalmatian lying in a snowy woodland beside the highway near where my friends and I used to go sledding.

These may sound traumatizing, or at least disturbing, especially to a young, impressionable mind. But they hadn't induced nightmares or phobias in me. Rather, they sparked my captivation with the morbid and macabre.

From an early age I loved Horror movies and creepy imagery. In my pre-teens I voraciously read Horror anthologies like *Shadows* and Horror comics like *Eerie*. As I got older, I became an avid fan of black comedy—Evelyn Waugh's book *The Loved One*, Hal Ashby's film *Harold & Maude*, the Butthole Surfers album *Locust Abortion Technician*.

I saved unusual murder articles from the local newspaper, like the son who killed his mother just because she would not make him spaghetti and meatballs for Thanksgiving dinner. I staged grisly crime scenes using stuffed toy animals. I mounted a paper banner on my bedroom wall that read "Necrophiliacs Like 'Em Cold." (Disclaimer: I am not, nor have I ever been, a necrophiliac.)

I was a weird kid, with very indulgent parents.

Now here I am today, all grown up with adult responsibilities, and I still haven't gotten that affinity for weirdness out of my system.

So that, dear reader, is what you're getting yourself into.

This collection of what I consider to be my best Dark Fiction short stories represents a twenty-five-year span of my writing career. As the author, it's interesting to review my works created over nearly half my lifetime. I'm obviously drawn to the darker sides of the human psyche. But I'm also intrigued by those who harbor secrets or suffer delusions, the faces they present to others often masking their perverse thoughts, feelings, or compulsions.

Hence the title of this collection you are holding, derived from Mark Twain's maxim found in *Pudd'nhead Wilson's New Calendar* (1897): "Everyone is a moon, and has a dark side which he never shows to anybody." It is a quote that resonates throughout the tales contained herein.

The Good Touch — This whimsical, irreverent story spawned from my newfound fascination with trailer parks, faith healers, and Jesus making His comeback on burnt slices of toast.

Cutting Remarks — My stab (or rather, bludgeon) at an *Alfred Hitchcock Presents* type of tale, one specifically inspired by a short story by Roald Dahl. There is nothing a married couple can't reconcile if they work it out together.

The Boy Who Cried Alien — I've always been a fan of '50s Sci-Fi alien/monster movies (see my anthology *What Has Two Heads, Ten Eyes, and Terrifying Table Manners?*). This is an homage to those films, and the people who watch too many of them.

Pet — Here is your typical "boy meets girl, boy loses girl, boy keeps girl's pet" Science Fiction story. It was inspired by the sad end of classic Hollywood movie actress Marie Prevost.

In Memoriam the Ostrich — Hypocrisy is one of my favorite themes. And cannibalism. What does the Bible say about cannibalism? Turns out, pretty much nothing. Which does not make the pastor's job in this piece easy.

The Mortality Machine — A love story of sorts that poses the question: if you say you'll love somebody forever, can you mean it literally? If you are a genius, maybe there's a way.

The Lord Is My Rocket — This is my satirical poke at religious zealotry, wherein the devout Christian caregiver of a developmentally disabled man vows to save his soul by taking him to a unique monastery. Moral: you can't save everyone.

The Beholder — The first draft of this character study about a man who finds beauty in everything he encounters was written back when I was in high school. Though edited substantially since then, all versions have retained its theme.

Mr. Gregori — In this Horror tale, a man cursed by a demon becomes infatuated with the new tenant of his apartment. Maybe she would love him in return… if only she could see, hear, or feel him.

FYVP — This is a nasty little teeth-clencher about body modification and those who get a thrill out of it, made a bit classier by the literary reference at its climax.

The Dark at the Deep End — Loosely (<u>very</u> loosely) based on some of my own teenage experiences, this *conte cruel* ("cruel tale") chronicles a budding serial killer before he acts on his sadistic impulses.

Suitable for Framing — With a plot salvaged from one of my earliest unproduced screenplays, it is a commentary on art, artists, and their fans. How much you enjoy this story perhaps says something about what kind of fan you are. Not judging; just putting it out there.

I hope readers will find these pieces entertaining. They are the cream of the rather limited crop of short works I've written to date, representing a warped window into my weird mind.

There are, I suspect, worse places to be.

–Sawney Hatton

THE GOOD
TOUCH

You'd think when Jesus did His encore, we'd get the whole enchilada, right? I mean, after a 2,000 plus year wait, He could've at least played us a full set with wicked sound and trippy lights and hot new moves we've never seen before. But as the angel explained to Les, the Lord is a very busy dude and has to divvy Himself up. Fair enough.

But damn... *this*?

Yeah, I know. I'm getting ahead of myself. Let's start with that night, when the angel paid Les a visit.

Me and Les were sitting in Les's trailer, pounding back a case of PBR, shooting the shit. I was bitching about the usual: being chronically unemployed and poor as a possum and still living in my mom's garage. Les groused about the Kiwanis canceling their annual bake sale for cancer kids.

Yeah, you read that right.

Les and me had been best buddies since grammar school when we'd bike over to Sawmill Creek to fish for perch. In middle school we drew superhero comics and played war games in the woods. In high school we partied with the chicks from Sunny Willow Girls School. Now it's ten years later and we Two Stooges (as Principal DeMott dubbed us) are still tight.

I'd like to think the reason Les still chums around with me is because he enjoys my company. But sometimes I think he just feels sorry for me.

See, compared to myself—who's always had this dirt cloud hanging over my head raining mud down on me— Les has the charmed life. He's the night manager at Stu's Market, getting paid enough to afford his own double-wide. He's got a 50" flatscreen TV with an Xbox 360. Girls say he's got a great smile. Everybody likes him. Not only is he sweeter than SoCo, he shows bottomless compassion for every living critter. Les is always willing to lend an ear to someone in distress, offer a hand to a worthy cause. He volunteers all his spare time during the day at the hospital, or the senior center, or the animal shelter. Joins those walks to find a cure for whatever. Guy's a friggin' saint.

So forgive me if I sometimes feel I'm nothing but a sinner in Les's eyes in need of saving.

Anyway, that night I tell him what I really need is a break.

He tells me I gotta want something to break into.

How 'bout a bank? I say. I was joking.

Les didn't laugh. Just gives me that "oh c'mon" face of his.

—

18

I then say I wanna win the lottery.

Les suggests I should come help out at the hospital. Or the shelter.

I say no. That would only bum me out more.

It'll make you feel better, he says. About my life, I guess. Make me less of a loser.

But I'd never be Les.

I tell him I'll think about it, but I'd forgotten all about it well before I drain my last beer. I leave his place sometime after 3 a.m. I walk home, take a leak in the bushes, crash out on my futon in mom's garage. The usual.

———————————

In the morning Les rings me on my prepaid cell. He sounds like he's buggin' out, begs me to come over right away.

My head's hammering and my gut's killing me, so I was in no mood for Les's burning puppy orphanage or whatever nonsense.

Is it *really* important? I ask him.

Mike, he answers, something happened to me last night after you left. Something mondo bizarro.

This stokes my curiosity. Of course he won't tell me what it is over the phone. He *has* to show me. So fifteen minutes later I'm back at his place. Les's face is paler than vanilla ice cream, and he's got this haunted, I-just-took-the-biggest-dump-in-human-history stare.

I notice he's wrapped up his left hand in a white T-shirt.

You hurt yourself? I ask him.

Les then tells me what happened:

"I was just dozing off. Or maybe I was already asleep. It was still dark out, I remember that. And then this amazingly bright light fills the room, as if somebody pulled a tarp off a searchlight in here. And then this light takes the shape of this long-haired, bearded guy in a white robe. Of course I'm like 'holy crap,' but for some reason I wasn't scared at all. The guy says 'Hello, Lester' and I say 'Who are you?' And he says he's an angel named Efram—no, I wasn't *that* drunk. I've never been so drunk I was seeing things— Efram tells me I am one of the chosen, that the Lord was giving me a special gift… a piece of Him. The angel told me a bunch of other stuff, mostly rules about using the gift. When I woke up, it was daytime, and I had this—"

Les unravels the shirt from his hand and shows me what it was covering.

My jaw drops and bounces off the floor.

Les had sprouted, between his thumb and pointer fingers, a sixth finger. It is almost a full inch longer than his tallest finger, and much darker than the skin of the rest of his hand. And it isn't sewed on or attached with glue or anything. It looks to be part of him, like he was born with it. He can bend and wiggle it by itself. It's perfectly manicured.

That's freaky, I tell him.

Les agrees.

So Jesus gave him one of His fingers. What for? I ask.

Les tells me it can heal people.

I'm skeptical. Why'd He pick him to get it?

The angel said he met certain qualifications.

Of course Les met them. As I said, guy's a friggin' saint. Still, I want to see proof of these special powers.

Let's check out what that freaky finger can do, I say.

We step outside and, as luck would have it, eight-year-old Billy Meijer had just fallen off his skateboard, scraping six inches of hide off his forearm. We find him bleeding and blubbering on the driveway neighboring Les's.

There ya go, I say to Les. Fix him.

He kneels down beside Billy and says some calming words to him. Tells him he's gonna try to make him feel better. The kid spots Les's coffee-stained extra finger and cries harder. Les tells him don't be afraid, it's his new magic finger. Then he touches the kid's raw wound with it and sure enough the bloody patch disappears like a magic trick. A miracle I guess you'd call it.

Wow! yells Billy.

That's awesome, I say.

Les seems impressed too. And kinda weirded out. Can you blame him?

I tell Les to do somebody else.

We trot over to Louise Bollinger's trailer. She's got emphysema and can't stop coughing. Magic finger does its work and POOF! No more hacking. Then we visit Eddie Frapper. He's stuck in a wheelchair, both legs crippled from a motorbike accident. POOF! Dude can dance again. Then we hit Sol Hockenfeifer's, who's blind. POOF! Sol can catch a movie tonight.

By end of the afternoon Les has healed the ills and injuries of all the citizens of Green Glades mobile park. We hear a lot of Hallelujahs and Praise the Lords. People weep, thank Les and hug him, offer him their cash and valuables (which he declines, being the good neighbor he is).

But that gets me thinking. This is our golden ticket, I say to Les. With his J-wand and me managing him, we'd be rich!

Les shakes his head. Can't, he says.

Why not? I ask.

It turns out to be one of the rules. He can't receive any payment for healing people. No money, no goods, no services.

I say, you're kidding me.

No, Les answers. The angel said if he breaks any of the rules, he loses His gift.

So what? I say. If you can't make a buck of it, what's the point?

Without missing a beat he says, I can help people.

Of course. It's Saint Les.

———◆———

When somebody has the supernatural ability to heal any-body's sickness or handicap, word about it travels faster than a hooker making the rounds at a political convention. Within a day, folks from all over town were pouring into Green Glades and lining up at Les's door.

Those with arthritis—POOF! Asthma—POOF! Heart disease or hemorrhoids—POOF! and POOF! Diarrhea, deafness, diabetes—POOF! POOF! POOF! All cured by the bona fide finger of Christ, retrofitted to my pal Lester Earl Tewlinski III.

I put myself in charge of crowd control, making sure Les's eager patients didn't try to elbow ahead of each other. Like Les, I wasn't getting paid a penny for it. But I had to admit, while not healing my undernourished wallet any, it was pretty exciting having a friend who could make people's lives better, who could save a life so easily. Everybody left his trailer happy and healthy and grateful. It was touching.

Dozens turned into hundreds by end of the week. They arrived from other towns, then other states, even other countries. Members of the Wrath of Angels motorcycle club signed on to help me keep the growing mob peaceful and orderly. We put up a chain-link security fence around Les's trailer and set up rope stanchions to corral everybody in the vacant lot next-door. Kicked to the curb anyone who tried to cut in line.

Fortunately Les kept things moving right along. Each person took at most five minutes inside with him. Better than waiting for a ride at Disney. And you didn't have to shell out a hundred bucks to get in neither.

The media started to swarm by the fifth day. First came reporters from the local papers, then from the tabloid magazines, then from the cable channels, then from the network news. That weekend even one of the hosts of "Good Day Nation"—the douchey guy, not the babe—had camped outside Les's home.

Loads of filthy rich people showed up too, from as far away as France and China. They cruised up in limos and Lamborghinis, all yearning for Les to treat whatever ailed them. All at no charge. Les couldn't even accept any gifts. If somebody left him something on the sly, like a diamond-encrusted watch or his own private jet (with personal pilot), he donated it straight to charity.

Les was really taking the rules seriously.

Me, I was looking for loopholes.

On Thursday of the second week, a pair of priests in purple capes and skullcaps dropped by Green Glades. Their first day there they just observed Les in action. On Friday they brought over this ugly Peruvian bastard with dry leprosy. Les did his mojo and POOF! Guy now looks more like the Crocodile Hunter than the Alligator Man.

The fancy priests must have reported the stellar results to their boss. The very next day the Vatican sent one of their bigwigs to our butthole town to meet Les. Bishop Sylvio had flown here all the way from Italy. He wore this sharp white suit with a shiny red tie and a shinier golden crucifix. He had the hair of an expensive lawyer and the teeth of an expensive dentist. He smelled like clove cigarettes. Sylvio also had this buttery Italian accent that could make a chick dampen her panties from across a room. He used it to tell me to leave him and Les alone awhile so they might discuss some matter in private.

So I waited outside with the other non-VIPs.

Twenty minutes later the bishop exits Les's trailer, marches over to his white stretch Hummer (without giving us unwashed masses—even the wealthy washed ones—so much as a "bless you") and drives off.

Les spends another hour and a half giving the folks finger jobs before calling it a day. I tell the five hundred plus people still in line to come back tomorrow at 11. As usual most stay put, not wanting to lose their places.

I ask Les what the bishop wanted.

The Pope wants Les to do a global healing tour.

Where to? I ask.

Everywhere, Les answers. Even the Middle East. They think he's the ultimate promotional tool for Christianity.

I see a problem. Wouldn't working for them be against the "rules"?

They talked about that too. The bishop said they don't have to pay him. They would just cover his expenses. It'd be like missionary work.

I decide that's OK. It'll be cool seeing the world. Let's do it, I say.

You can't, Les says softly.

I ask him to repeat himself.

Les looks me in the eye, all sympathetic, and says I can't go.

Why not? I ask.

The bishop told him I didn't adequately represent the Vatican's image. Guess he meant I wasn't religiousy enough.

I should've been pissed, but Bishop Sylvio was right. I'm not religiousy at all. I'd probably embarrass myself on the road. Get drunk in Australia. Get high in Amsterdam. Get laid in Japan. Get in a fistfight in Russia. I'm a horrible role model for anybody, much less Christians.

Les, though, isn't all that much better. Sure, he's nice as nookie, but he's no king of the righteous. He drinks and smokes and screws nearly as much as I do. And Les was never the churchgoing sort neither. He only thanks God for stuff now and then (Thank God for weed!), more often damning other stuff in His name (Goddamn shoelace!). I'd wager most any preacher has superior credentials. Hell, lots of the folks in line could probably make a stronger claim for being holier than him. In my opinion, Les didn't deserve to sport Jesus's finger. Maybe the angel had made a mistake.

I wanted my best friend back.

More than that, I wanted that magic finger. Badly.

So I finally figure out a loophole.

Les was jetting off to Rome Monday afternoon. I come over Sunday night to help him pack. I bought us a cheap bottle of rum for a bon voyage party. I pour us each a glass and slip a few roofies into Les's.

For the next twenty minutes before he conks out we talk about normal stuff. Nothing about his world tour, or the Pope, or even his frankenfinger. Just shit we did together in high school—smoking grass at MacArthur Park, throwing M-80s in the boys room toilets, double teaming Amy Gratzen. Good memories. Made me kinda sad.

Once Les passes out cold, I use my mom's gardening clippers to cut off Jesus's digit. It's more of a bitch than I thought it'd be. (Not that I'm any expert on chopping off fingers.) I have to put my full weight on the clippers before the finger snaps off. I plunk it in my jeans pocket and split.

Now I could go around healing folks myself. And since I wasn't bound by any heavenly contract like Les was, I *could* get paid for it. Or, I could skip all that grind and sell the finger to the highest bidder. Must be worth millions. Hundreds of millions! I'd be set for life. I could buy my own castle in Scotland. Gather a harem of hoochies. Eat clambake every day.

Yeah, guilt chewed at me. But greed fed me more.

I doubted Les would ever forgive me, but I hoped he'd understand. Sometimes opportunity doesn't knock. You have to break in.

When I enter my bedroom/mom's garage, I put her clippers away on the wall where they belonged. Then I chug a beer from my mini fridge. Then I puke in the toilet. Then I reach into my pocket… and scoop out only greasy black dust.

Jesus's finger had disintegrated.

———————⚜———————

Les wakes up the following day with a monster headache and minus one magic finger. The wound I'd made healed up overnight. There isn't even the tiniest scar. It's like it was never there.

Les seems to take everything in stride. He calls to tell me first. Next he phones Bishop Sylvio and informs him of the situation. Les then goes outside and announces to his faithful followers that his trip is off, that his healing powers have been revoked, and that he is very truly sorry.

Nothing twists the heart more than the sight of scores of sick and lame folks who've had their hopes crushed. It takes nearly two hours for all of them to drift away, shuffling or limping or rolling back to their regularly scheduled lives.

Much like Les and me did. Les went back to managing Stu's Market. And I went back to chilling out with my buddy who didn't have an extra finger belonging to the son of God. Our life is as it was before, everything as it should be. I almost thanked God for it.

Except I'd also learned I got stage 4 stomach cancer and had, with chemotherapy, maybe a year or two to live. Without chemo, maybe a few months.

I don't have insurance, so I guess I'm on the fast track to Game Over. I haven't told Les any of this because, well—

What do you think I did wrong? Les asks me while we polish off a case of PBR and play *Grand Theft Auto 5*.

Dunno, I say.

I followed all the rules, Les groans. Every. Single. One. Maybe he could contact the angel—

I cut him off right there, saying maybe it was because he got too famous.

Les mulls this over then says, You mean fame was a form of payment?

Yeah, I answer. Could be. Probably.

Les sighs, sags his shoulders. He seems to accept my explanation. He then says Efram should have been more specific, insists he could've saved so many more people. Hundreds. Thousands.

I feel the tumor pain in my gut again. I rub my belly, wincing.

You alright? Les asks.

Just my ulcer acting up, I answer. Ulcer. That's what I told Les I had.

I could've done something for that, he says, when I had the… y'know.

Yeah, I say.

I knew.

———

CUTTING REMARKS

Two of Sinclair's teammates knock on his front door that rainy Saturday afternoon, after he had missed his Friday bowling night twice in a row. They had tried calling his house numerous times, but the phone was apparently, oddly, off the hook.

"Oh my, yes. That's true," his wife Hedda confesses, embarrassed. "I didn't want its ringing to bother him. You know if Sin doesn't get enough sleep he can be a real crabapple to deal with!"

Hedda straightens the strap of her green sundress and brushes strands of prematurely graying hair from her face. She invites them (*such nice men, Hedda thinks*) into her home. "Please, sit down a spell. Would you like some coffee?"

They enter and wince. The stench, potent and putrid, is unmistakable.

They find Sinclair in the couple's king-sized bed.

"Shhhhhh," Hedda hisses at her husband's friends. "Don't wake him. He so needs his rest."

———————

It had been dinner as usual and there was that bitter taste in her mouth again, scarcely five minutes after she had sat down at the table to eat.

Mind you, it was not the meal. Hedda's cooking was unanimously praised in town—she often contributed to potluck suppers at church functions—and tonight's chicken cordon bleu was no exception. A superb dish.

No, the source of her distaste was her husband of eight years. Sinclair. She once thought his name, and the man himself, to be so dignified, so sophisticated, even exotic. Now to hear his name spoken made her skin squirm.

And the sound of his voice made her throat tighten like a tourniquet.

Sinclair was, as some described him, a critical sort. Scornful was more accurate, by Hedda's reckoning. He relished expressing his not-so-humble opinions to anyone who would lend him an ear. Beyond that, he was keen to provoke, to rouse a heated reaction from folks, even if he himself knew he was just spewing a lot of hot air. And since he, a retired electrician, seldom ventured out of their small—too small—cottage home anymore other than to go bowling Fridays, Hedda bore the brunt of her husband's antagonism.

He didn't care to debate politics or sports with her like he did with his Ten Pin Bowl buddies. Rather, he threw a barrage of verbal darts at her, about her, and the deeper they stuck, the better.

"Your arms are getting flabby."

Building muscle, they were, from keeping up the house.

"You're looking old."

Of course, at age 42, she was no pompom girl, yet she still had her admirers—oh, that flirty Mr. Milford at church!—but being a good Christian, she never gave into temptation.

"Don't you ever have anything interesting to say?"

She did. Since her third miscarriage three years prior, he hardly ever listened anymore, so she had given up trying to make conversation.

"Do you plan on moving your lazy butt to do something 'round here today?"

She toiled for him and his home twelve hours or more each and every day. Didn't she deserve those precious few minutes watching her favorite TV programs?

"You are worthless, woman."

Hmmph! See if he could live without her!

"You make me sick."

Oh, how she loathed him.

"This food ain't fit for starvin' dogs."

It was this last remark that finally impelled Hedda to crack Sinclair's skull with the metal meat-tenderizing mallet. He slid off his chair and crumpled beneath the table, without a fuss, which was very unlike him. But he wasn't a particularly robust man. Quite delicate actually. Hedda was almost twice his size and strength. But it was always the scrawniest runt with the biggest mouth, wasn't it? Trying to compensate for what he lacked in physical prowess. If only somebody long ago had clobbered him for talking too tough, too smart. All those aches and bruises from being beaten with fist and foot could really have left an indelible impression on one as tiny and as loose-lipped as Sinclair Koppinger. But nobody had ever taught him the virtue of respecting others.

He had learnt his lesson now, Hedda was confident.

Sinclair twitched a moment, then moved no more. A crimson pool spread underneath his head. She would have to mop the linoleum soon before the stains set in.

There was something pathetic about him, she mused. This proud bastard of a man sprawled on the floor like a broken puppet. Very sad indeed. Hedda lifted her husband up and, cradling his limp body in her arms, carried him to bed.

Quite a change overcame Sinclair since that evening. He no longer snored like a revving bulldozer. (*Ahh, Hedda couldn't remember when she had last slept so soundly!*) He paid far more attention to what she had to say. Most gratifying of all, he didn't cut her down anymore, didn't berate her, didn't belittle her. Suddenly, the noxious burden that had been her husband was swatted from her weary shoulders. She was unshackled. Free.

The following days were, in a word, delightful. Hedda watched all of her afternoon soaps without interruption, as well as two game shows and a funny sitcom. She baked a tray of oatmeal raisin cookies for herself. She played her chorale hymns album on the living room record player, loud enough so she could hear it in the kitchen. She did not vacuum the carpets on Tuesday as was her routine; no doubt they could wait until Thursday, or Friday. She solved a crossword puzzle, sewed a button back on her prettiest dress—Mr. Milford said she looked positively angelic in it—and treated herself to a warm Epsom salt bath. As always, she attended Mass on Sunday morning, then went grocery shopping afterwards.

And all the while, Sinclair was, if not appreciative, certainly acquiescent.

It was heaven. Hedda was able to allow herself to relax again, and to thoroughly enjoy it, without worrying about Sin barking at her and disturbing her newfound peace of mind.

Even Pastor Greeley commented on, so out-of-the-blue, how happy and contented she seemed.

Well, Hedda replied to him, she had recently been the beneficiary of fortunate circumstances. It was like a divine thunderbolt had struck her, and she felt—yes she was—saved. Then Hedda smiled, without elaboration.

She hadn't smiled for ages.

When Sinclair awoke, Hedda couldn't help but feel an overwhelming wave of disappointment.

She'd been watching one of those true crime shows, which had only recently become something of an addiction for her. Her heart pounded and her stomach churned when Sin stepped into the TV room, glared at her, and grumbled, "I'm hungry. Make me something."

Gone was the towel that Hedda had wound around the crown of his head. There seemed not a drop of blood on him. In fact, his head appeared wholly unscathed. (*And she had bashed it in good!*)

Curiously, he didn't mention Hedda's assault on him. Maybe the blow had impaired his memory. Maybe he was toying with her. Regardless, he had reverted to his usual habits.

Hedda rose from the sofa to go make him his favorite sandwich—ham and Swiss on rye with mustard. Sin stood right beside her at the kitchen counter, eyeing her with disgust, his hot breath wafting down her neck. She concentrated on tuning out his voice, but his big mouth seemed to have grown, literally, bigger. Amplifying his every pricking, prodding utterance. He hollered and bellowed and roared, and it rattled her bones. His words burrowed into her flesh and clawed at her insides.

"What a surprise! You sitting on your rump."

Take two slices of bread…

"Been fattening your belly more I see."

Two slices of ham…

"You look like crap."

One slice of cheese…

"You dimwitted, good-for-nothing, poor excuse for a wife."

And a dab of mustard…

"G'damnit, woman! Don't you ever speak up?"

Her composure withering, then shattering, Hedda glowered back at him and shrieked into his face:

"SHUT UP!"

Sinclair appeared stunned by her outburst. So was she. It was very unlike her.

She blinked and swallowed. Her throat tingled.

He shrugged and huffed. Vehemently, defiantly, he answered her: "No."

It then occurred to her, maybe there was no way to shut him up, or shut him out. Sin was a stubborn man by nature and demanding anything of him was akin to lighting a fuse to a never-ending string of dynamite that would explode over and over again, longer and louder, wreaking more damage with each and every blast, until…

Hedda began to sob.

Sin smirked at her.

There was no relief. No escape.

Unless… she pondered.

Yes. The idea was so simple, so sensible, how could she not have thought of it before? It just hit her, like a thunderbolt. A moment of inspiration that would set her free, and put him in his place, once and for all.

She grinned.

"No? Well, dear," she crooned, gazing at her husband, dead in his eyes. "I'm afraid that won't do. Won't do at all."

———◆———

It is a week later when the policemen (*what handsome boys they are, Hedda thinks, in their spiffy blue uniforms*) come to examine Sinclair Koppinger's body tucked snug in the bed, decomposing in the dank air of the room.

He had been decapitated—several days postmortem, it was later determined—his head neatly sawed off.

That part is uncovered, with Mrs. Koppinger's polite cooperation, in the yard, buried in a shallow patch of soil along the stockade fence. (*A fine spot for a vegetable garden, she chatters to the officers.*) Mr. Koppinger's cranium is caved in, his mouth stuffed full of cotton balls, then duct taped over.

"It was the head, you see," she explains. "That sour-puss of a brain connected to that yappity flappity mouth. Indeed, it was Sin's head that was spoiling our marriage.

"But things are much better now since the separation, thank you."

THE BOY WHO CRIED ALIEN

Jeremy Martin was ten years old when he learned extra-terrestrials had replaced his parents.

His family lived in West Olchester, an unremarkable northeastern town composed of cookie-cutter post-World War II tract homes (Jeremy's father was a veteran) and a Main Street worthy of a Norman Rockwell painting, lined with small mom & pop stores showcasing weatherworn signs and bright American flags and Christmas lights in their windows year-round.

Jeremy's father worked as the sole proprietor of a leathersmith shop (named "Leathersmith Shop") specializing in hats, vests, and gloves. His mother was a homemaker who baked a scrumptious Dutch apple pie, a favorite at church socials. Jeremy was their only child, as much child as they could afford on Mr. Martin's modest income. But it was enough for Jeremy, who seldom wanted for anything, save for the fulfillment of his fanciful dreams.

Throughout the 1950s—a wondrous and terrifying period for stoking a kid's imagination—Jeremy and his friends frequented the single-screen movie theater on Main Street, often sneaking inside through a rear door that didn't shut properly unless the ushers remembered to slam it.

From the front row they watched scores of Westerns and Thrillers and Adventures, but were most captivated by Science Fiction's aliens, spaceships, and strange planets, most of these hostile to Earth's human denizens. The boys also enjoyed fantastic-themed TV programs like *Superman* and *Space Patrol*. They read comic books galore, marveling at the latest exploits of superheroes battling supervillains from this world and beyond.

These were simpler times, when a child could plainly distinguish between good and evil.

Until Jeremy discovered one can hide behind the other.

The day his life changed forever, Jeremy had caught his fourth matinee of *Invaders from Mars*, about a boy who uncovers a plot by space aliens to take over the minds of all the grown-up Earthlings. Afterward, Jeremy bought the newest issue of *Superman* ("in startling 3-D") at the five & dime and went home. He dashed upstairs—his mother yelling behind him, like always, "No running up the stairs! You'll trip and break your teeth!"—and into his room, throwing himself onto his bed and diving into the comic. He read until suppertime.

Dinners at the Martin household were regimented affairs. His mother would call him down, often while he was in the middle of doing something else he'd rather be doing than eating with his parents.

"In a minute!" Jeremy would answer.

"Now!" his mother insisted. "Don't make your father come fetch you!"

Jeremy never let that happen anymore, not since his dad started giving him the buckle end of his belt.

The atmosphere of every family meal was cold, formal without reprieve. It was a time to reinforce the values instilled by Jeremy's parents, both God-fearing, freedom-revering Americans, with Mr. Martin especially embracing the role of not only patriarch but of patriot.

"How was school today, son?" he'd ask after grace.

"Fine, sir."

"How is your food, son?"

"Good, sir."

"What is the last vestige of hope for a free world?"

"The U.S. of A., sir."

"Amen."

Television was forbidden after dinner. That time was spent gathered in the den, where Jeremy's father read aloud from the daily paper articles about active threats to the United States, or any news across the globe which might pose a menace to it in the future—communism, fascism, rebellion, disease, technology. The Martins needed to be informed, prepared.

Mr. Martin had built an underground fallout shelter in their yard. Mrs. Martin had taught Jeremy to cook for himself and tend to his own wounds. Nothing would have made his parents prouder than for their son to serve his country, to protect it, better yet (Jeremy suspected) to die for it.

It had been a convincing ruse.

That fateful night, unknown to his parents, Jeremy stayed up well past his bedtime to view a meteor shower from his window through his Unitron refractor telescope, a Christmas gift from his Aunt Dorothy whom he hated. He loved gazing into the night skyscapes. He dreamt he would someday travel to the stars, seeing things no man has ever seen before, exposing the mysteries of the universe. He fancied himself a future space detective.

By midnight, Jeremy's drowsiness surpassed his interest in the cosmos. Before getting into bed, he stepped out to relieve himself. (He'd already brushed his teeth and washed his face earlier at his mother's behest.) He had to pass his parents' bedroom on his way to the bathroom down the hall. Ordinarily he found their door shut. That night, however, it was slightly ajar, and Jeremy could hear vaguely human moans inside.

His curiosity uncontainable, Jeremy peeked through the door crack into the darkness.

As his eyes adjusted to what meager light was produced by his father's alarm clock and the street lamp that bled through the curtains, he could discern lying on his parents' bed two reptilian-humanoid creatures covered in scales and polyps, their saurian mouths drooling, their spindly limbs entwined.

Jeremy froze, stifling a gasp.

The larger of the monstrous pair rose into a kneeling position. It flipped its smaller confederate onto its hands and knees facing the headboard then scooted up behind it. A stiff tendril a few inches in length extended out of the larger creature's abdomen and inserted into the base of the smaller creature's spine. For several moments, they varied the depth of the protuberance by rocking their pelvises back and forth. Both made groaning, grunting noises during the process.

Jeremy raced back to his room, leapt into his bed, and cowered beneath his blankets without even noticing he had peed his pajamas. He remained there until he was sure they hadn't spotted him, weren't coming for him.

He realized at once what they were: aliens.

He caught them in what might have been some act of organic information exchange. More significant, he caught them out of disguise. For reasons unknown, they had taken the place of his parents. These creatures treated Jeremy as if he were their own child, with never a false note played, for how long he hadn't a clue. Weeks? Months? *Years*? It boggled his mind.

The boy had stumbled upon what was undeniably part of some fiendish plot against the Earth. Now he had to figure out what to do about it.

———◆———

What Jeremy did about it was wait.

Up to that point, the aliens had been clever, maintaining their human appearance whenever he was around.

Now that he knew their secret, he could orchestrate ways to watch them unawares.

It became Jeremy's sworn duty to find out why they were there and what they had done with his real mother and father. This was a rescue mission—not just for his parents but perhaps for the entire world. A lot of responsibility for a young boy to bear, yet who else could do it?

Jeremy took to spying on the aliens whenever they thought he wasn't home, or was asleep, or otherwise preoccupied in his room. Once, through the copper keyhole of the bathroom door, he beheld the smaller creature brushing its jagged fangs in the mirror, its jaws slathered in foam. On another occasion, he glimpsed the larger one late at night standing in front of the refrigerator, gorging on the carcass of the leftover roasted chicken the family had for supper. Particularly curious was when Jeremy witnessed this same being in their garage under the hood of the station wagon, tinkering with its engine just like his father would. He speculated the alien was rigging the vehicle with some sophisticated technology to make it fly, should the impostors require a hasty escape if their plans for conquest were thwarted.

Jeremy perpetuated his role as their son, pretending to be well behaved, ignorant. He shared meals with them as usual, helped his "mother" clear the table as usual, and listened to his "father" presage potential perils impacting America as usual. Jeremy continued to let them throw parties on his birthday for him and his fewer and fewer friends. (He had told none of them about his situation, worried this knowledge would put them in danger too.)

He even continued going on vacations with the impostors to the lake every summer, though his constant vigilance prevented him from having much fun.

Jeremy, while not trusting them, was not very concerned they would hurt him, as they had not done so already. He'd been careful not to give them reason to.

He *was* concerned that he hadn't gotten any closer to the truth of what their agenda here might be. The aliens had assumed his parents' identities uncannily well, revealing nothing useful to his investigation.

Eventually Jeremy was able to recognize subtle cracks in their characters. Mother never seemed comfortable in her adopted body, always fixing her hair or adjusting her skirt. Father developed a habit of peering out the living room blinds, as if checking for something amiss on or around their property. And sometimes they would take the car out for an hour or two to run errands together, yet they often returned without any items—groceries, for instance— that would account for where they had gone on their trip.

"Where'd you go?" Jeremy would ask.

"Sightseeing," father always joked (because there were no sights to see in West Olchester). And mother typically said they had been at the church or the bank.

Jeremy made attempts to follow them on his bicycle, only to lose them after they rounded the first corner at the end of his block. He had observed both their church and their bank. Mother and father were never at either place. He wondered if they were instead rendezvousing with their home world superiors somewhere, maybe in the secluded hills south of town.

Jeremy had called the police and the local Army recruitment office, but they didn't believe him, telling him that if he didn't quit fooling around he would be in a lot of trouble.

He tried photographing the aliens in their true form with his dad's Kodak Brownie camera, a task difficult to accomplish on the sly, resulting in a half-dozen dark, blurry shots substantiating nothing.

Undeterred, Jeremy kept waiting and watching, ever prepared to complete his mission to save his parents and his planet, whenever and however the opportunity presented itself.

There came the time when waiting and watching was not enough, when decisive action needed to be taken before it was too late.

Jeremy had just turned fifteen. His "parents" threw his birthday dinner at the Silver Spoon Diner. It was only the three of them. Jeremy had invited none of his friends, who by then were not so much friends as they were classroom acquaintances. They didn't even sit at the same lunch table anymore. Mother and father gave him a model kit of the Juno 1, the rocket that had launched America's first satellite the year before. Jeremy thought they were patronizing him.

"What're your goals this year, Jeremy?" mother asked him.

"I'm gonna save the world," he answered.

His parents traded wary glances with one another. Jeremy thought he had given himself away.

"How do you intend to do that, son?" asked father.

Jeremy shrugged. "I'm not sure yet."

Father chuckled at him. "Well, you let us know when you suss it out. We'll be happy to help."

Jeremy nodded and continued eating his ice cream sundae. Playing dumb seemed to have worked in allaying their suspicions.

Upon arriving home, Jeremy bounded up the stairs to his room. He stowed the rocket model box, unopened, inside his closet. For the next hour, he studied the waxing gibbous moon through his telescope, mapping its craters in pencil on a sheet of loose leaf paper.

When he had grown bored with this, he surveyed his neighbors' houses, peering into the windows of illuminated rooms, comparing the lives of others to his own. He envied most of them, the loving families, the laughing children. Sometimes he effortlessly pictured himself among them. Other times it was like watching a TV show being broadcast from a thousand miles away.

The Sterns lived behind the Martins, the rears of their virtually identical houses facing each other. Arthur and Edith Stern attended the same Methodist church as Jeremy's parents. The young, always smiling couple had visited their home on a few occasions, whenever Jeremy's mom hosted one of her potluck Bible study brunches. They seemed like decent folk as far as Jeremy could tell. Mr. Stern once pulled a magic coin—a shiny nickel—from Jeremy's ear. Mrs. Stern told him more than once he was such a handsome boy. The Sterns did not have any kids, which Jeremy felt was a shame. He imagined they would be good parents.

Jeremy could see the Sterns through their bedroom window, on their bed. Except it wasn't the Sterns. It was their substitutes, shed of their human facades, engaged in their strange and grotesque mode of information transfer, a variant of the technique practiced by his replacement parents. One creature was mounted upon the other. The top undulated its lower abdomen against that of its bottom counterpart, which wrapped its tentacles tightly around the other's torso, probably to maintain their connection. Their scaly, gator-green skin glistened.

Jeremy knew immediately what this meant. The alien presence was not an indicator of an impending full-scale attack, not a mere reconnoiter operation to gauge human vulnerabilities. Rather, this was a colonization already in progress. West Olchester, or at least the West Olchester Methodist Church, had obviously been compromised. And who knew how many more towns, cities, or countries had also been stealthily, systematically infiltrated? It did not bode well for Mankind.

Jeremy needed to do something. But what *could* he do? Nobody took him serious. (And who could he actually trust now anyway?) He was just a lone, lanky teenaged boy versus a cunning, hostile race of technologically advanced imperialists from another world.

He felt dazed and helpless and scared.

No matter how he felt, Jeremy knew he may well be Earth's only hope.

But again, what could one person do?

———

What have heroes throughout history done in the face of oppression and degradation?, he pondered.

They rebelled.

Like all the brave people—farmers, students, artists (and, in the comics, Superman)—who resisted the tyrannies of the Nazis. Like Sitting Bull, who used his prescient visions of victory to embolden a confederacy of Indian tribes to defeat Custer's cavalry at Little Big Horn. And like Jesus Christ, who single-handedly expelled the moneylenders from the temple.

Yes, Jeremy would fight back. He would spark the Earthling Rebellion.

And it would start under his roof.

———⊶⊷———

Jeremy waited in his room until 2 a.m., when no creatures were stirring in the house. He collected the things he wanted to keep—some clothes, a stack of comic books, his telescope (minus the tripod)—and packed them in the Army rucksack his father had brought back from the war.

Jeremy then got the can of kerosene from the basement and the matchbox from the top kitchen drawer. He snatched the framed photograph off the wall in the foyer, the one of Jeremy standing in front of the house with his mom and dad before their supplantation.

This was for them, wherever they were now. And for the U. S. of A., the last vestige of hope for a better world. And for all the heroes before him who had made the ultimate sacrifice. Amen.

Jeremy stood in the front doorway, struck a match, and dropped it onto the doused hardwood floor, touching off a wave of fire that swept up the stairs and quickly engulfed the landing leading to his parents' bedroom door.

With the rucksack slung over his shoulder, Jeremy sprinted across the street and hid behind a maple tree. Monitoring his house from there, he could see swarms of orange flames whirling and flailing behind the windows downstairs. Within moments the blaze had blown out the glass and scorched the hedges. The American flag hanging beside their stoop was reduced to cinders in seconds.

Against the moonlight, Jeremy spotted dense, dark billows of smoke pouring from the chimney. He could smell it too. He expected the upstairs rooms to soon be assailed, the invaders from space incinerated in their sleep. The first battle won.

The dormer window to his parents' bedroom shattered outward. Father was breaking it with the base of a brass lamp. When the frame was cleared of shards, he clambered out and assisted mother onto the roof, then onto the ivy-clung trellis on the side of the house. The creatures had the presence of mind to change back into their human guises and don their Earthling nightwear. They climbed down the flimsy wood latticework. Jeremy prayed they would fall and snap their necks, but they made it to terra firma safely.

He had not accounted for the possibility they could escape. He scolded himself for the oversight.

Mother wobbled on her bare feet, coughing harshly, her eyes rheumy. A gash on her right heel bled. Father led her away from the conflagration and laid her down on the lawn near the driveway.

Alarmed neighbors streamed from their homes and approached. Mr. Bowers, who owned the hardware store on Main, brought over a first aid kit and tended to mother's wounded foot.

"Jeremy!" father wailed. He frantically scanned the growing crowd. "My son… Has anybody seen my boy?"

"He's right here!" somebody answered.

People parted to let Jeremy through.

"Thank God," father sighed. He gazed down at his wheezing comrade. "Sweetheart, Jeremy's alright." Swelling sirens pierced the night. Somewhere a dog barked.

"Everything's going to be alri—"

Jeremy clubbed father's skull with his telescope three times before someone behind him seized his arms. He heard his last hit make a satisfying wet crunch.

"Stop it, kid!" shouted the man who held him. "Are you crazy?"

Jeremy stared at father hunched over mother, his hands cupping his scalp. Blood dribbled from between his fingers. He whimpered like some wretched animal.

The boy struggled to free himself, to finish what he had begun.

"They're aliens!" he screamed, over and over, until his throat burned and his mouth frothed.

Jeremy figured he had been in the room for two, maybe three months. He'd thought it would have been a faster trip. Their home planet must have been very far away.

His cell was small, even smaller than his bedroom on Earth, its walls painted a powder blue, with a single entryway and a skylight. The door was always kept locked (they never let him roam the ship unsupervised) and the skylight was secured with thick metal bars (though he couldn't reach it anyway). The furnishings were spare too—just a bed, a nightstand, and a desk and chair. No closet. They brought him fresh clothes and three meals daily. And the white pills to make him a more docile captive.

Jeremy presumed he'd been replaced by one of them on Earth. He wondered what would happen to him on their world. Science experiments? Slave labor? Zoo exhibit?

Whenever the human-clad aliens entered his room, he'd ask them how much longer would he be in there. Until the doctors believed he was well enough to be discharged, they told him.

The "doctors" met with him a few times each day. They would ask him why he did this, how did he feel about that. Jeremy told them nothing but his name, school grade, and street address. He was a loyal soldier. He knew his mom and dad would be proud of him.

Every night, Jeremy looked up through his skylight, at all the stars that never seemed to get any closer, trying to guess which one he was bound for.

PET

"Every living thing requires something on which to feed in order to live. A pet depends on its master to feed it; therefore it is the master's burden—at its most fundamental—to maintain the pet's life."

Jusita Lu Yeffar, COO
Mhurian Empathy for Organism Welfare
(MEOW) Int'g

Pinky's master is Stacia Moz, perhaps the brightest and positively the prettiest roprogrammer at the Gamma-One Automaton Designworks. She has natural blonde curls and double-dimpled cheeks and the beautiful ovoid eyes characteristic of native-born Pyzureks. And her body, flawless by all current standards in the Mhuri Galaxy.

Stacia is, as they say, *hot as Hoggra!*

Her boyfriend Dex ranks only a Level C-5 Engineer in Gamma-One's Exo-Skeleton Department—he failed his

C-4 certification twice—but he is handsome, charming, and devoted. Good enough for Stacia, most of their fellow plant workers agree. (And even those who don't can understand the attraction.) By all appearances they are a well-matched couple.

Stacia and Dex had met in the south wing commissary at lunch during the summer. He accidentally spilled her jollup juice. Not only did he buy her another cup, but also a cocoanut pudding, which she shared with him.

By autumn, they'd moved in together into a luxury skyrise apartment in downtown Trivicon City. He made her breakfast every day, and she made love to him every night.

They were happy then.

———◆———

Stacia was never allowed any pets growing up at her parents' home on Nabaru, because her papi did not ever think she was responsible enough, and her mums was allergic to near about everything anyway. Stacia had told Dex again and again how she'd always wanted a pet of her own. He got the hint.

He bought the creature from an interplanetary trading freighter and brought it home as a birthday gift for Stacia. Commonly called a fluffox (its zoological name is ridiculously long to spell and near impossible to pronounce), they are popular companion animals among the upper castes, prized for both their docility and cuteness.

A fluffox most resembles the brindle-fleeced head of a male Wixian lion, minus the snout. Its eyes are large, round, and rheumy—adorable sad puppy eyes. Lacking the prototypical mammalian mouth, it can only ingest liquid nutrients through the hairless, sea anemone-like stalk protruding from its shaggy face. It also has bird-like feet, and bald rosy-hued hindquarters much like the baboons of Earth. For this reason Stacia named it Pinky.

Stacia plays games of fetch with Pinky and its vulcanized toys whenever she has the spare moment. She takes it out for short conveyor-walks, cleans up after it, scolds it when it misbehaves. And she feeds it, mostly scrowz milk, but occasionally treats it to snow viper broth if she remembers to pick up a carton from the market.

In contrast to Stacia, Dex is not much of an animal person. He has never really liked Pinky. But he likes how much Stacia seems to like it. That's enough for him.

For a while it was anyway. Dex scarcely bends a finger to help care for the creature. *It's your damn fluffox*, he tells Stacia. *It's your job to take care of it.*

Taking care of Pinky eventually becomes too taxing a chore for Stacia. It constantly grovels for food and whines for attention. It knocks things over, messes the floors, wakes her up in the middle of the night.

Some of Stacia and Dex's coworkers believe this was the spark that had lit the fuse to what ultimately detonated their relationship.

But most think Stacia was just too good for him. They could never last.

Nobody is quite sure when his boozing began, but a year after Stacia had settled down with him, Dex was terminated from the Gamma-One plant. He had a tough time finding alternate work and soon gave up trying. Instead he aimed to drink himself every day to the brink of insensibility, until he could feel nothing anymore.

Nothing but anger.

Dex often comes home battered and bruised from starting fights at the local saloons with whoever happened to provoke him that evening for whatever reason.

He raises his fists to Stacia if she nags him about it. Or if she tries to calm him down. Or if he just has the urge to strike something.

One day Stacia decides to break it off with Dex. She no longer loves him, she tells him as the transporters haul her stuff from the apartment. She is fed up with his raging and rampaging. He's unambitious and lazy and worthless. She doesn't see a future with him.

Dex begs for her to stay. Promises he'll change. Yells she'll regret dumping him. Smashes a full bottle of ninety proof Krevvar against the wall.

Unswayed by his pleas, Stacia departs Dex's life.

And leaves poor Pinky behind with him.

Three days later, Dex staggers over to Stacia's new place of residence. He's learned she has become romantically involved with Mr. Bogg'ins, the Vice President of Sales at Gamma-One, and now shares his uptown manorplex.

Dex bangs on the front door. Bawling, he asks for her to forgive him, to please come back, to give them another chance.

Mr. Bogg'ins calls the constables on him.

I need you Stacia, Dex sobs as they escort him, wrists shackled, into the raptech cruiser. From the backseat, he looks out at the expensive home, his eyes ricocheting from one window to another. He never sees her.

A night in the drunk cell humbles Dex.

From then on, when all the saloons have closed for the day and he returns to his lonely home and crawls into his empty bed, all Dex craves before drifting off to a fitful sleep is to hurt something as badly as Stacia hurt him.

———✕———

Pinky naps in its corner by the photonic stove. Dex sits at the kitchenette table, finishing off a Quilq eight-pack. He glares at the fluffox flopped on his floor. He is already sick and tired of filling its feeder and wiping up its muddy poop.

And yet it is the last thing he has that connects him to Stacia.

Oh how he misses her.

Now that she's gone, maybe it's best to get rid of the hairy beast. Ditch it on the crossway. Let it fend for itself. Or get whacked by a jetbus. Whatever.

Dex rises from his chair and looms over Pinky. He sets the sole of his foot on the creature's head and slowly applies pressure. Pinky's big eyes widen, then wince. It scratches at Dex's chaffan pants and squirms its plump body, struggling to wriggle out from under his djarvian leather workboot. He pushes down harder. The creature is trapped there, at his mercy. He wants to crush it. He wants to see its brains burst from its skull.

But when Pinky whimpers pitifully, Dex lifts his foot. It scurries away, cowers beneath the kitchenette table.

Dex lights a cigarella, tries to think about nothing.

⸻

The next night, Dex arrives home earlier than he usually does—though still much later than most people who work regular daily shifts—his nose busted and his bottom lip split from another brawl. He slams his door shut upon entering.

Pinky, sniffing at a dead myl beetle, swivels toward Dex, alarmed.

Dex kicks the creature, launching it across the room. It hits the bookcase, bouncing off and rolling halfway over the parlor rug. It scampers into the bedroom, hides beneath his bed.

Dex laughs, licking his bloodied lip.

⸻

The following morning, Dex chases Pinky throughout the apartment, gleefully flinging knives and tines at it. It darts under his bed again, panting and trembling.

Dex flips on the Tel3V and plops into his lounger to catch the end of *The Greco Granite Show*.

Dex has not fed Pinky for a week now. While he is out at the saloons, it digs through the kitchenette waste bin for any rotting food soft enough to consume. It also learns to suck up the green mold growing along the baseboards.

Twice a day, if he remembers, Dex leashes the creature on the balcony where it can do its business. Often he leaves it out there for hours, even in the rain, until it whines and howls and scratches at the sliding window. Once he gets annoyed enough, Dex will let it back inside.

Pinky always runs away from him.

On Wednesday, or Thursday—does it matter anymore?—Dex brings home a bag of cheap Oongolese food. He sits down at the kitchenette table, eating from the styroweave containers.

Pinky observes him intensely, its stalk wagging, saliva dripping from the tip.

Dex, enjoying his meal, ignores it.

The creature pounces onto the table, overturning a box of biomac stew. It spatters onto the floor. Pinky leaps down and siphons the gravy greedily.

Dex smashes his fist down on its spine. Pinky grunts, then whips its stalk out and snatches the barbecue woplings from the tabletop. Dex attempts to grab them from it, but Pinky honks at him and dashes under the bed, slurping up the sauce, watching him with wary eyes.

Frik you too, Dex grumbles.

———————✳———————

Another day. After going through a pack of Quilq ale and a book of cigarellas, Dex rises to use the lav.

He discovers Pinky perched on the toilet bowl rim, drinking from the basin.

With the palm of his hand, Dex shoves the creature down into the water. He holds it under the surface until the air bubbles taper off. He then yanks it up and hurls it into the shower pod beside him.

Pinky gasps for breath as Dex relieves himself.

Grinning, he blows cigarella smoke in its face.

———————✳———————

Dex is almost out of funds on his savings stick. He's already pawned most of his furnishings except the bed, lounger, and Tel3V. Any money he has left he spends on cigarellas and penny liquor from the quick-shop.

He can't afford the saloons anymore. He is five days late paying his rent. They had shut off his visiphone the week before, and yesterday the power company sent him a FINAL NOTICE memtron.

Dex figures he'll just bail from his apartment right before they jiglatch his entry lock. He will then live in the shelters, or on the streets, surviving by his wits. Free of all obligations.

He pops one of his porn-x cards into the media slot on his Tel3V and, wearing nothing but a pair of dirty white boxies, leans back on the lounger. He takes a swig from his last bottle of Krevvar and gazes at the viewer screen.

Soon Dex begins touching himself. How long has it been since he plugged a fem? Too frikkin' long. His passions swelling, he desperately wants release, but his hand refuses to bring him the gratification he so much desires.

His nethers ache. His mind burns.

Dex glances over at the fluffox, lying feebly by the front door. Focuses on its bare pink rump.

That's why she named it Pinky.

Oh how he loves Stacia still.

Still aches and burns for her.

And she had once loved him. And Pinky.

Aching and burning.

Pinky never hears him approaching.

Dex straddles the creature from behind, seizes two clumps of its fur, and hoists it from the floor. He then sinks himself into her.

Pinky shrieks like rusty whirling gears.

Dex closes his eyes, plunges deeper.

Stacia... I love you... sooooo much...

Pinky's stalk flails. Its talons claw the air.

I!

Love!

You!

Dex peaks spectacularly.

———

He collapses onto his bed sometime after midnight, passing out whilst staring at a crack zigzagging along the ceiling. It reminds him of a lightning bolt, far away and fleeting.

Dex awakens to a flash of pain.

Sharp tiny nails dig into his chest, a warm weight pressing down on him. He groggily opens his eyes to see Pinky's face in front of his own, looking at him.

It is a little known fact—one certainly unknown to Dex—that a small percentage of fluffoxes possess a second vestigial orifice approximately two inches beneath their stalk. When feeling extremely threatened or stressed or angry, they may pry apart the fused flesh to reveal a fully functional gullet and a mouth sporting a broad set of jagged teeth. Meat-eating teeth.

Pinky smiles at Dex.

Then sinks its jaws into his throat.

A week elapses before the building manager, Mr. Zevnök, comes to check on his tenant Dex, who reportedly has not been seen for days. And the month's rent is way past due.

Mr. Zevnök uses his passpunch to gain entrance. He calls out Dex's name as he creeps into the apartment.

The fluffox greets the lessor, hopping excitedly and tooting its stalk. Zevnök pats its head, notices a brownish crust matting its muzzle. Disgusted, he wipes his hand on his trunks.

"Mr. Volga?" he hails again.

With the fluffox following on his heels, Zevnök surveys the kitchenette, leisure room, lav. Nobody.

Finally, he inspects the bedroom.

He peers into the dimly lit space from the hallway. It takes a moment for his vision to adjust, to recognize what he's seeing. There on the gore-soaked bed is what remains of Dex.

The pet has been well fed.

IN MEMORIAM THE OSTRICH

Everyone on the island showed up that morning for the reading of Professor Thacker's last will and testament, though not everybody stayed until the end. Most did. But not all.

Pastor Higgsby was one of two early departures. Not even the crisp briny air could assuage the nausea churning his belly. As Thacker's final wish went against God and basic morality, the clergyman was especially affronted. Almost as disturbing, the majority of the townspeople seemed to be considering it.

Pastor Higgsby was now certain. Thacker had had the Devil in him. Which wasn't really surprising. He had had lots of things inside him at one time or another, much to the delight of his fellow islanders.

"Are you alright, Pastor?"

Pastor Higgsby turned away from the sun-glistened bay and faced Ewan Mavensmith, lifelong fisherman and oldest inhabitant of Edessa Island. Everything about him was thin—arms, legs, torso, neck, lips, hair—and while well into his 80s, and looking every year of it, he remained as sharp and spry as someone half his age. He smoked a carved bulldog pipe.

"Yes. I'm fine," Pastor Higgsby answered the patriarch. "Just needed some fresh air." He spotted Lania Cox, bless her soul, disappearing over the knoll in the distance on her way home, away from that abominable assembly.

"Lovely day, aye?"

"It is." The pastor cleared his throat. "Did you leave early too?"

Mavensmith shook his head. "The reading's done. Everybody's just sorting out the details."

"So then… they're all on board with this?"

"Well, I wouldn't say everybody's quite cozied up to the idea yet, but it *is* Professor Thacker's last request. Seems disrespectful to deny him it, and it won't hurt nobody none. Besides, it seems right fitting, don't you think?"

Pastor Higgsby found his whole body had gone rigid from outrage, which made sense for him as a disciple of the Lord, but surely the others would come to their senses and recognize the depth of depravity they were being compelled to undertake. God help them if they didn't.

Professor Thacker professed to have once been an instructor at Fausbröt University, teaching global economics. He never presented any proof of this, but that did not matter to the islanders. Thacker was a very wealthy man who retired to Edessa a decade ago, purchasing Gowie Manor on the northern bluffs, and ever since then had spread his wealth among the locals. Daily he bought their homemade foodstuffs and their homespun clothing and their hand-made crafts, and he bought them all drinks every night at Vernon's Olde Tavern. Yet Thacker had not only been beloved for his generosity. He possessed a unique ability, a curious talent that had endeared him to most.

Thacker was a Human Ostrich. There must be a more proper term for it, the pastor presumed, but that was the carny-given nickname that Thacker had used as well. Like an ostrich, Thacker, who was not a particularly stout man, could eat most anything—coins, keys, silverware (including knives), jewelry, shoes, buttons, bones, stones, glass, rope, hooves, once even the Celtic cross off the tavern wall—and he regularly performed such feats of extraordinary in-gestion to the perverse amusement of the citizenry.

"Are you sure you're all right, Pastor? You look awful pale."

"No, Mister Mavensmith," Higgsby admitted. "I am most definitely not *all right*."

Thacker had been thoroughly self-serving and self-aggrandizing, exuding enough brash confidence to humble the holiest of men. Truth be told, Pastor Higgsby had dis-liked the man from their first introduction—he caught him plucking crocus blooms from the rectory garden—and only grew to detest him more and more with each encounter thereafter. Thacker was never a churchgoer, declaring with haughty irreverence that Sunday was *his* day of rest (though Higgsby had never seen him doing much of anything the other days of the week either). He was a glutton, a lush, a boor, a hedonist, a heathen. And now, even in death, he further orchestrated his spiritual degeneracy and designated the islanders his accomplices.

The crime—and surely it *must* be illegal—they were about to partake in was the partaking of Professor Cornelius Thacker himself. Within twelve hours of the will reading the residents of Edessa were to prepare, cook, and consume the deceased. If they complied with this, the sum of his fortune would be divided up amongst them.

The professor had been very shrewd indeed in his postmortem plans. For one, the short duration he allotted for the islanders to decide allowed no opportunity for any law-abiding dissenters to report the obscenity to the mainland constabulary. For another, Thacker appealed not only to the citizens' greed, but also to their ingrained goodness.

"If you care for each other as much as I hope you'd cared for me," his will read, "I know you deserving folks will use the resources from my estate to help one another attain the rapturousness and righteousness God wants you all to have."

It was this blasphemy that had driven Pastor Higgsby out of the meeting hall. Recalling every deviant, diabolical word of it, he left Mavensmith to his pipe and returned to the rectory.

Higgsby prayed for hours.

He prayed for strength for himself. He prayed for counsel from the Lord. He prayed for redemption of the islanders, his flock.

The pastor could not figure out where he had failed them. Since his appointment to the island's parish thirty years ago, every resident of Edessa (excluding Thacker) attended his sermons religiously. They all believed him when he pronounced he could guide them onto God's path and into the Kingdom of Heaven. They had faith that he could illuminate the Lord's words so they would see His light. They listened to him, they learned from him, they let him tend to their very souls. And in less than a day all that would be shunted aside to yield to the whims of their false idol.

Pastor Higgsby felt forsaken. Hurt. Defeated.

No! He wouldn't surrender! He realized he was being tested. God was always testing the devout. Higgsby likened it to the quality check of a life-saving device.

He vowed he would save them.

The pastor marched over to Vernon's Tavern. Brown ivy clung tenaciously to its exterior. Inside, most everything creaked—the floors, the tables, the chairs—but these were seldom heard above the din of rowdy drinkers. Many of the islanders were gathered there now, quaffing ales and wines, some already quite soused.

Higgsby asked Oakley, the barkeep, about the status of the sordid affair: Patsy Dunkirk, the town doctor and undertaker, had butchered the professor's body. The pub's proprietors Chip Klausen and his one-armed wife Bethilda had sliced, seasoned, and seared the meat, and at that very moment were simmering it—him—in their largest cast-iron pot in the kitchen. Thacker was being made into a stew, his favorite dish. Pastor Higgsby could *smell* it.

He stepped up onto a pinewood chair and called for everyone's attention.

"I implore you, my brothers and sisters of the Lord Our Father, do not defile yourselves by committing this wicked act!"

"Gettin' sloshed," said Ewan Mavensmith, "seems a right tribute to pay to one's passing."

"I don't mean the imbibing. I mean… the dining."

"But it is the Professor's last wish!" somebody yelled from the rear, somewhere by the mounted boar's head.

"It is a sin!"

"Is it?"

"Yes, Horace," who was sitting closest to the pastor, "cannibalism is a sin." Higgsby was astounded he had to point this out, even to one as dull-witted as Horace.

"Didn't the Apostles eat Christ's flesh 'n' drink his blood 'n' whatnot?" remarked Chip Klausen, taking a respite from cooking the evening's main course.

"That was symbolic! And completely different!"

"Ah. 'Cause Jesus were still livin'," said Zena Worley, the town midwife.

"Pardon?" replied the pastor.

"Jesus could give His consent bein' alive and all. It made it more legal-like."

"The Professor gave us consent in his will," somebody else chimed in.

Everyone nodded and drank, as if that settled everything.

"That's not it!" Higgsby shouted. "Nobody actually ate His flesh or drank His blood because *that* is a *sin*."

"Then why the hell did He even bring it up then?" Chip asked. "Seems a weird bit to be chattin' about over supper."

The pastor took a deep breath. "We're digressing. I am telling you, as the one who has ministered your church for thirty years, that consuming human flesh is a very, very, *very* grievous transgression in the eyes of God. Each and every one of you, as Christians sworn to uphold the Gospel's principles, you *must* abstain from going through with this... atrocity."

"But tell us, where exactly in the Good Book does it say cannibalism is wrong?"

"Thacker's a Godless man!" Higgsby blurted. "And we are blessed to be rid of him!"

The room fell silent.

The pastor's eyes darted from stony face to stony face. They all stared at him, judging him. Higgsby knew he'd misspoke. One does not speak ill of the dead, even if one is a man of the cloth. Especially then, perhaps.

Ewan Mavensmith spoke on behalf of them all. "We can respect your opinion, Pastor, if you can respect ours."

Higgsby stepped down from the chair and steadied his hands on a table. He averted his eyes from the crowd.

"No. I cannot."

"Then maybe it be best if you kept to yourself today, 'til our offense to your sensibilities is done with. And I think we can all promise, out of respect to you, this day'll never be mentioned in your company again."

Everybody nodded. Resigned, the pastor nodded as well and turned to free himself from that den of iniquity.

———

"See you on Sunday, Pastor," Mavensmith said, quite pleasant.

Higgsby paused at the door, palpitating, his back to his congregation.

"Aye," somebody else said. "We all will."

The pastor left.

———————

It was getting dark, and the moon glowed faintly though the swelling clouds like a dying lantern. There was a whiff of brimstone on the breeze. Or perhaps that was just the pastor's imagination.

Higgsby scarcely recognized them now. Mavensmith, Oakley, Patsy, and the others sullying their precious souls at Vernon's. People he had known for decades. Some he had even baptized! They appeared sinister in the tavern's lamp-light, with shadowy eyes and crooked grins. They had all been bewitched by the Devil, Higgsby concluded. A Devil who went by the name of Thacker.

Only upon reaching the crossroad on his way to his parish did the pastor remember he was not the only one who had retreated from Thacker's will reading. Lania Cox had bailed from the hall before Higgsby had even sprung from his seat.

Miss Cox was a pretty, fair-haired maiden of twenty-two who in all her years had never missed a service of the pastor's, even after both her parents died from pneumonia.

She always sat in the front pew in her simple white dress, listening to the Pastor's every word, the Holy Book open in her lap (though she seldom looked away from his pulpit). Lania loved the Lord and was plainly enamored with Pastor Higgsby, the Lord's vessel. She often baked him honey tarts.

At least she would be saved!

He needed to see her and commune with her, let her know she was not alone.

Lania answered her door in a simple black dress. Her eyes were red and rheumy. She threw her arms around the pastor's waist and hugged him for a long while, her face buried in his chest. She trembled.

"Are you alright, Lania?"

She gazed up at him and said in a cracking voice, "He's gone."

The pastor looked down at her, bemused. "Pardon, dear?"

"Poor Cornelius."

"Thacker? You are upset about Thacker?"

Lania nodded and sniffled. *She was mourning him!*

"I'm so grateful you're here, Pastor. I must confess something."

Lania invited Higgsby inside her thatched cottage. It had only two rooms, a spacious living area consisting of the kitchen, dinette, and parlor, and a single bedroom in the rear. A portrait of Christ hung on the wall above the stove. Lania kept the place tidy and scented with roses and cloves. Higgsby noticed the dining table had been set for two.

Lania wrung her hands and paced the length of the table.

"What do you want to tell me, Lania?"

She eased herself into a dining chair, in front of one of the place settings. "Last night I made him his rabbit and potato stew." Lania stared down at the unused plate, gilt rimmed, painted with floral flourishes. "I made sure everything was perfect... I think he was going to ask me to marry him."

Pastor Higgsby could hardly articulate the revelation. "You... and Thacker... you were..."

"We were in love." She began sobbing again.

Higgsby made no move to comfort her. He yearned to flee, to pretend this was all a delusion, or damn it all if he could not.

And then he glimpsed the gold through the gloom.

The pastor filled the empty chair opposite Lania. "I understand that you had harbored affections for Mister Thacker," he said. "But that's not your fault. Your feelings were the product of temptation. Thacker could tempt a turtle out of its shell." (To eat it, Higgsby thought wryly.)

He smiled at her. "It was not love, Lania. It was lust. Lust for companionship. Lust for sweet nothings. Lust for another's touch. I know how terribly lonely you must have been, you poor girl. How lonely you may be now. But you still have the Lord. And me."

Lania had not really been listening. Her mind was elsewhere.

"Lania?"

"My womb," she finally said, "bears our fruit."

"You... you're pregnant?"

She nodded.

"Nearly five months. Cornelius was so happy. So excited." Lania gasped. "You don't think that's what caused his heart attack?"

"I… don't… know…" The house suddenly felt much warmer to Higgsby. He felt woozy.

Lania sighed. "Suppose it doesn't matter. It was God's will. But I will honor his memory by raising our child to be as kind and gentle and good as he was."

The words reverberated in Higgsby's mind: *"raising our child."* Thacker's child. A child that would no doubt also be nurtured by the misguided people of Edessa Island. A child Lania would want the pastor to christen. A child borne of the Devil.

Her eyes drifted to the stove, and she smiled dreamily to herself. "After the delivery I shall sup on the afterbirth. Cornelius told me they do that in China… for good luck I think… And it's very nourishing… I'm thinking of a nice shepherd's pie—"

Higgsby had stopped listening. A tempest whirled and crashed in his skull. He stood and stumbled out the door, staggered down the pebbled path, and shambled across the soggy fields toward the bluffs. Here the night swallowed everything: the town, the trees, his own hands. He could not even see the sea.

He could still hear them. The wind carried the merry sounds of fiddles, flutes and drums, of drunken laughing and drunken singing. The island had embraced the profane spirit of the occasion. The meal was underway.

His flock was feasting.

Pastor Higgsby had lost them all.

———

He peered over the cliff edge, down at the surf-swept rocks he knew to be far below, and wondered if God would forgive him.

THE MORTALITY MACHINE

"Come, Lilah! It's ready!"

When Lilah entered her husband's workroom he was still tinkering with the machine.

"You said it was ready an hour ago, dear."

"Well, it's definitely ready *now*, hon."

We'll see, she thought.

The machine didn't look like much. Just a big steel box with lots of switches and dials and gauges, plus this weird antenna thing on top that resembled a Whirly Pop. Todd had told her it was made of five different rare metals. She didn't recall the names of any of them, but then her memory wasn't what it used to be.

No doubt about it, her husband was a genius. Before he retired Todd had been an astrophysicist and before that a bunch of other scientific job titles she hardly understood. She didn't understand what he had invented now, only that he was building it for the both of them.

"Won't you come have dinner?"

"Dinner? No time for that. This is too important!"

Lilah sighed in disappointment. She'd cooked them a delicious leg of lamb. She always enjoyed having dinner with Todd out on their veranda, with its spectacular view of the sunset behind the mountains. There was a time he wouldn't miss it for the world. Now his world was all about that darned machine.

When the cancer spread into his bones, the doctors gave Todd only six to nine months to live. He'd bested that prognosis by a year. He attributed it to keeping busy, an idle mind being the surest route to a body's surrender. Still, he was so much thinner now. Weaker.

"Please, dear. It'll get cold."

"No time, Lilah!"

She hated when he barked at her, a far more common occurrence since he'd gotten sick. They'd recently celebrated their 45th—or was it their 46th?—wedding anniversary, but spent most of that day in separate rooms instead of dining out or going dancing or making love as they had in years prior. She couldn't contain her resentment.

"Why is that silly thing always more important than spending time with your wife?"

Todd turned to her, his face at first manic but quickly melting.

"I've told you why, hon. Many times… Don't you remember?"

Lilah, a trifle embarrassed, shook her head.

"That's alright. I can explain it again." His tone was heartfelt and patient.

"We've talked about out-of-body experiences, right? That's when a person's so-called soul or spirit, when they are in an altered state of consciousness such as in a deep trance, separates from the body and drifts uninhibited through any spatial dimension. This device allows us to channel our psychic energies to consciously control this astral travel. Since we'll have no tangible form or substance, we'll possess absolute freedom of movement."

Lilah nodded and smiled. Her husband could tell it was beyond her.

"Once we exit our bodies, physical deterioration will no longer be a concern to us. Death is no longer a factor. We can elude it."

"We wouldn't die?"

"Exactly! And we can be together forever."

"That would be cheating death then?"

"Not cheating. Revising the rules."

"We'd be ghosts?"

"We'll be living on a different plane of existence."

"But what happens to our bodies?"

"They become irrelevant. They won't house our consciousness anymore."

"But… they'll still be alive."

This notion disturbed her.

"Well yes, they'll carry on their metabolic functions until they naturally break down. But our bodies are really nothing but shells. We, the vital part of us that makes us who we are, won't be with them to further suffer the ravages of aging, to become victims of mortality. By departing this material world, we become immortal."

Lilah was not an especially religious woman, yet what her husband proposed did seem some sort of blasphemy. Playing God, she believed the phrase was.

"So… we'd be cheating death then?"

Todd gazed at her, teary-eyed.

"We'll be together forever. Everything like it was before. Won't that be marvelous?"

Lilah nodded slowly. She wondered what time the sun set today.

"You're working so hard, dear. You must've worked up a hunger. Why don't we go eat, enjoy this lovely Spring evening? That machine will still be there when you get back to it."

"We're ready, Lilah. Why wait?"

"Please, Todd."

"Let me do one more test run to check the pineal flux calibrations. Give me fifteen minutes, thirty at most. Then we'll eat. And after dinner we can go together. You'll love it. You'll see."

Todd was like a child on Christmas morning, Lilah thought, with a brand new toy he needed to play with this instant. Nothing else mattered. Despite her exasperation, Lilah didn't want to begrudge her husband any satisfaction over his accomplishment. Of course he was excited. She supposed she could entertain his whims for a half hour.

"Fine," she said. "If it'll make you happy, take it out for a spin."

Lilah watched her husband prepare himself for his otherworldly jaunt. After he verified all the machine settings were correct, Todd climbed into the nearest of the two beds he had placed next to it. He fitted a swim cap on his head that had a bunch of wires leading from it into the machine. In his hand he grasped a remote control.

Once everything was in good order Todd smiled at his wife.

"Be right back."

"I'll be waiting," Lilah answered.

Todd pressed a sequence of buttons on the remote. The machine hummed to life, the needles of its gauges fluttering, its antenna lighting up with crisscrossing electric waves. Her husband then shut his eyes and within a couple of minutes he was gone. Like he had just fallen asleep.

The machine beeped in sync with his heartbeat.

Lilah putters around the kitchen, wiping down the counter-tops, running the disposal and replacing the dish towels. She keeps the lamb warm in the oven, but worries it will dry out soon.

No matter—she can roast up another. She takes the opportunity to get some more cleaning done, washing and dusting and vacuuming. She picks the ripe tomatoes and green beans and lettuces from the backyard garden. Finishes her latest Sudoku puzzle book. Crochets a shawl for these chillier Autumn days. Even goes to church, where she hasn't been since Easter.

"It's wonderful to see you, Lilah," the pastor tells her.

She tells him she'll try to come more.

The pastor says her husband is always welcome too.

"Thank you," Lilah answers. "Todd has just been so very busy with his work. But I'm hoping it won't be like that for much longer."

She feels a twinge of guilt by her reply, like she's part of some conspiracy, helping her husband play God. Yet Todd simply yearns for them to be together. Surely God would not find any fault with that.

Todd still sleeps. He looks more gaunt now, his skin more gray, which Lilah attributes to his advancing illness. She changes out his clothes and briefs regularly. She feeds him nutritious broth twice daily, helping him swallow by massaging his throat, a trick she'd learnt from her nursing days.

The machine still beeps. She thinks this is good.

At the grocery store, Maury, the butcher, asks her how her husband is doing.

"Todd's fine," Lilah says. "He's away."

"Good for him. Where'd he go?"

"Oh yes but he'll be home soon thanks Maury," she gushes, grabbing the wrapped leg of lamb and dashing off. Todd told her not to tell anyone about his machine. She's proud of herself for remembering that.

In a bedroom drawer she finds their wedding album, full of faded pictures capturing beautiful moments between the blurred spaces in her mind. There are so many people in them she no longer recognizes. But without a doubt, that was Todd, her love, her life. For better or for worse, in sickness and in health, until death would they part.

And she knows Todd is not dead.

He still beeps.

"How is Todd?" their neighbor Jane... no, Joyce... asks Lilah, stepping out to fetch the mail. "I haven't seen him at all lately."

"He's been a bit under the weather."

"Well, I hope he feels better."

Lilah thanks her and hurries inside the house. The mail is mostly bills, something Todd always takes care of. She wishes he would come back to her.

She thinks she hears him call her name. She rushes into his workroom.

"Todd?"

He doesn't respond.

Still, he beeps.

Every day she reads to him, sings to him, holds his hand, strokes his head. Every day she dresses nice and fixes her hair for him, as she'll be the first thing he sees when he reopens his eyes. And every day before dinnertime, she sits at her husband's side and waits, hoping he will return in time for them to share one more sunset together.

Just one more, Lilah prays.

WHITE SPACE

(A TALE OF AURAL TERROR)

The blizzard wailed like a banshee in labor.

EVERYONE IS A MOON

Paul pounded on the ancient door. "Kevin! Are you in there?!"

All he could hear was the wind whipping him.

Kevin groaned.

Paul tried to scream, only choking on the unrelenting snow whooshing down his throat.

THE LORD IS MY ROCKET

Ruth Greenaway coasts her yellow Kia Spectra to the mouth of the narrow gravel roadway, flanked by woodland so dark she'd almost missed it. Her headlights shine on the gold-lettered sign:

MONASTERY OF THE CELESTIAL CHRIST

Visitors welcome with reservations

Ruth switches on the car's interior dome light and consults her *Divine Places* magazine, the leading publication for Christian destinations.

"This is the place. It got a four-cross rating in here. Sounds like it will be right up your alley, Floyd."

The prim woman smiles at her young ward, who keeps squinting out the windshield at the canopy of stars above. He wears a pair of bulky headphones, plugged into the Fisher-Price cassette player set in his lap. Ruth again hears The Marcels's *Blue Moon* coming through the padded speakers. It must be the twentieth time the song has played on their trip here, along with the other doo-wop tunes on the mix tape Carla had given him the year previous. It is all Floyd has listened to ever since.

Ruth drives a half mile up the remote road before they reach the cloister. She parks the car in its asphalt-paved lot beside a gray passenger van, the only other vehicle there.

"C'mon, Floyd. Your salvation awaits!" He scrunches his face as if someone had just blown into it.

The bulk of the building is shrouded in murk, except for a spherical, stained-glass sconce resembling the planet Saturn lighting the rustic wood entry door. They approach it, Ruth nestling her Bible beneath her arm, Floyd clutching his cassette player to his chest.

A knotted rope dangles by the door. Affixed to the wall beside it is a small white placard that reads, "Pull To Summon."

"I guess we tug this to ring the doorbell," Ruth says and does so. There is no sound. She pulls it once more and presses her ear against the sturdy door. She still hears nothing within.

"Maybe it's broken."

"Pull harder!" Floyd shouts, manically grabbing the rope and yanking it over and over and over again, as if he were trying to win a prize in a carnival game.

Ruth grasps his forearm. "Stop that, Floyd. It doesn't work—"

A panel behind the door's speakeasy grill slides open, revealing part of a monk's scowling face.

"I heard you the first time! One pull is all that is required!"

"Sorry," the startled Ruth says, her palm patting her pounding heart. "We didn't hear it ring."

"Perhaps that is because it rings on the inside," the monk sneers. "You are standing outside. Do you ring to summon yourself?"

Ruth apologizes again.

"Never mind. What is your business?"

She recovers her composure. "We come seeking enlightenment."

"It's rather late for that," the monk says.

"Pardon?"

"It's after eight."

"Oh," Ruth falters. "I didn't know you closed."

"We do not close, miss. But, we do value common courtesy, as uncommon at it may be these days. Do you have reservations?"

"No, sir."

The monk growls in irritation.

"We do not accept any guests without making prior arrangements. Call in the morning, but don't expect a room to open until next month. We are full now."

"Please excuse my ignorance," Ruth beseeches him. "But we have traveled quite a long way, and we have no place to stay tonight."

"I said we are full. I cannot help you. Call tomorrow. Or don't. It's your choice. Goodnight."

The monk slams the panel shut.

Pursing her lips in frustration, Ruth jerks the rope.

The monk appears again at the grill, gritting his teeth. "What is it?"

"You don't understand." Ruth looks him straight in his one visible eye. "This is a spiritual emergency." She then leans even closer to him and whispers, "There might not be a tomorrow."

A few minutes into the meal, Floyd's nose started bleeding into his milk.

Ruth's regular Tuesday second shift at the Fairchild Home for Adults with Special Needs had begun uneventfully enough. She arrived at work about ten minutes late, as usual. (Carla quipped she must run on "Biblical time, before they had clocks.") After relieving Laura, the daytime caregiver, Ruth minded the facility's seven current residents—Debra, Floyd, Gregory, Lizzie, Peter, Rebecca, and Victor—while her coworker Carla prepared dinner. The four men and three women varied in ages from early 20s to late 50s, with varying degrees of mental disability that necessitated them to be institutionalized.

A converted Victorian-modeled manor that once belonged to a newspaper publisher, the Fairchild Home was one of the nicer places Ruth had worked in, retaining many of its original 19th century fixtures and frippery. These lent it an air of godliness, Ruth thought, that reminded her of a historic church rectory.

There were even angel figures carved into the crown moldings!

Since graduating high school ten years before, Ruth had served as a special needs caregiver, initially as a volunteer, then as a vocation upon earning her certification.

The job didn't pay much—just enough to cover her studio apartment rent, utilities, and semi-ascetic lifestyle—but its other rewards were of greater import to Ruth. Whenever she had the opportunity, she would read her charges passages from her leather-bound King James Bible, her most treasured possession. The book had belonged to her mother, and Ruth carried it with her everywhere to honor her Mama's memory and her life's mission to spread the Good Word to all who would listen (and an equal many who would not).

"You know they don't really understand what you're saying, right?" Carla had once remarked after walking in on one of Ruth's impromptu spiritual storytimes with the residents.

"They're listening," Ruth replied.

"You mean they hear you. Maybe someone catches a word here, or a word there. But it's all probably mostly gibberish to them."

"You don't know that for sure."

"I'm pretty sure you're wasting your time."

"Salvation is never a waste of time."

"No?" her coworker countered. "And what if you're trying to save someone who don't wanna be saved?"

"It's not a matter of *want*, Carla. I only have to open the door, and the Lord will take it from there."

Carla shook her head, suggesting—again—what Ruth really needed was a man in her life.

"I have a man. The greatest man who ever lived and died and was"

"Resurrected," Carla finished Ruth's stock phrase. "Hope you two lovebirds are very happy together."

The evening God imposed His will on Floyd, and by extension Ruth, they had all sat down at the master dining room table for a meatloaf, mashed potatoes and mixed vegetables supper. Ruth recited the customary grace, with everyone bowing their heads, even Carla. Much like firing the starter pistol at a race, as soon as she uttered "Amen" forks dug into food. Victor, the youngest resident at the home, meticulously segregated each item on his plate before taking his first bite. Lizzie hummed "Happy Birthday to You" while she ate, though it wasn't anybody's birthday. And Rebecca, their most impaired ward, only kept wiggling all her fingers in front of her eyes until Ruth pretended to sprinkle "magic yummy dust" on her meal.

"Y'hear China sent more of their battleships into the Pacific?" Carla said. "What ya wanna bet, with us distracted with that, the Russians gonna invade some of them tinier countries in East Europe—"

"Carla," Ruth interrupted her. "That's not appropriate dinner talk."

"What?" Carla wrinkled her nose. "It's news."

"It's bad news, not to be discussed at the table."

"Fine," Carla sighed. "That David Radcliffe was on Conan last night."

"It's Daniel," Ruth corrected. "Daniel Radcliffe."

Gregory began chanting "Radcliffe" over and over. Ruth hushed him.

"Whatever his name is, he's hot stuff."

"I heard he's an atheist."

"I think he's Jewish," Carla said. "Wipe your mouth, Peter."

Peter, one of the group's messier eaters, blotted his gunky lips with his napkin before shoveling more potatoes into it.

"Whatever he is, I won't watch his movies."

"You saw *Harry Potter*."

"We all saw that together. And it wasn't my choice."

"Uh oh," they heard Floyd squeak across the table.

Ruth and Carla directed their attentions to him.

Blood poured from his nostrils into the glass beneath his chin, turning the milk he was drinking pink.

"Oh, Christ!" Carla cried out. She and Ruth sprung from their chairs. Carla slid the glass away from Floyd while Ruth pressed a napkin to his nose and tilted his head back, knocking his NASA cap off.

"OH MY GAWD!!!" Debra blurted. She spun around, squeezed her eyes shut, and rocked her forehead against the wall. Gregory mimicked her exclamation. "OH MY GAWD! OH MY GAWD! OH MY GAWD!"

"Quiet down, Gregory!" Carla told him.

"Did he hit himself somehow?" Ruth asked.

"I don't know. Maybe?"

Ruth gingerly lifted the napkin from Floyd's face. Blood still trickled from his left nostril.

"It's not stopping."

"We better get him to Saint Luke's," Carla said.

"I'll take him." Ruth instructed Floyd to continue holding the napkin to his nose. She then guided him by the arm out of the house and into her car.

"You'll be OK, Floyd," she said, buckling him in.

"Uh oh," he answered.

———— ◆ ————

The surly monk introduces himself as Brother Guiseppe. Ruth guesses he is in his forties, showing the first strands of graying hair at his temples. Garbed in a shimmery black satin robe, he leads them down a broad, dimly lit corridor.

Lining the monastery walls are backlit celestial images featuring moons, stars, planets, and nebulae. Above them hovers a giant mobile of the Milky Way galaxy (Floyd was able to identify it), with a larger-than-life-sized statue of Jesus Christ in a shepherd's frock suspended amongst the spiraling cosmos, posed as if He were flying through it. Like Superman, Ruth thinks.

Floyd, mesmerized by the colorful panoramas, slows to study them. Ruth prods him forward to keep pace with the monk, who doesn't seem to care whether they are still behind him or not.

"We really appreciate you making an exception for us," she says in an effort to ingratiate herself.

"I do not have the authority to make exceptions," Brother Guiseppe responds coolly. "Only the Abbot can overrule our protocols. And then only if the circumstances are extraordinary."

"I think he'll see they are."

"There's nothing extraordinary about dying, miss."

Ruth worries Floyd overheard the monk's insensitive comment. But her ward, still fixated on his surroundings, seems quite oblivious to all else.

They reach a mahogany door adorned with a large bas-relief of a dove in a space helmet. Mounted at eye-level beside it is a gold plate engraved with the name of the chamber's prestigious occupant: *Abbot Mortimer, OSB.*

"Wait here," Brother Guiseppe tells the visitors.

The monk enters the Abbot's quarters. Ruth and Floyd take a seat on a marble bench next to the door.

"Don't worry, Floyd. The Lord watches over us, and will open any doors that'll lead you to His Pearly Gates."

Floyd fiddles with the buttons on his cassette player and again listens to *Blue Moon*. Ruth modestly buttons up her ecru linen dress to the collar and primps her strawberry blonde bouffant. She then swipes some dangling strands of Floyd's fine brown hair from his brow.

Brother Guiseppe re-opens the door moments later, beckoning them inside with an impatient wave. "Come. Abbot Mortimer will see you."

"See?" Ruth says to Floyd after removing his headphones. "Jesus opens doors for you."

"Thank you Jesus," Floyd says to Brother Guiseppe.

In stark contrast to the classic rich woods they have seen throughout the monastery so far, Abbot Mortimer's office boasts decidedly modernist materials, with sheets of brushed steel layering the walls. From the ceiling juts a square bank of glowing bulbs on silver stems, resembling an inverted light garden. The Abbot's desk is topped with kaleidoscopic glass in the shape of an artist's palette, with an "Italian Futurism" inspired (according to the Abbot) aluminum frame/chair hybrid. On the wall behind him hangs a number of framed articles, puff pieces and reviews of the monastery that had been snipped from magazines and newspapers.

Ruth sits in a multi-angled, vinyl-upholstered chair opposite Abbot Mortimer. Across the room, Floyd kneels slack-jawed before an alcove, fascinated by an illuminated sculpture of a spinning sun hewn from yellow crystal. A miniature Jesus figure stands stationary within its hollowed-out center, the sun ceaselessly revolving around Him.

Ruth explains their special situation to the Abbot, omitting only those details that may rouse complicating concerns. He wears the same fashion of robe as Brother Guiseppe, but with an added embroidery on its breast—a white, five-pointed Star of Bethlehem. Designating his title, Ruth supposes. She reckons him being in his mid-fifties, his solicitous expression and well-groomed hair reminding her of Reverend Covington, the parson of her childhood church.

Ruth was six years old when the good reverend had announced the Blessed Virgin Mary would appear atop a peak in the Black Hills on Assumption Day, and that great favors would be bestowed upon all those who witnessed the miracle. On the appointed date, more than five hundred believers, including Ruth and her mother, traveled to the foot of the mountain and spent the day staring into the sky. (Truth be told, little Ruth spent much less time staring, but rather worked on erecting a small dollhouse out of stones.) Her mother, along with the rest of Covington's devout flock, gazed into the blazing sun, waiting for their Lady to appear. Consequently, many pilgrims sustained a loss of their vision. But Ruth's mother had never lost her faith, for in fact she had seen the Divine Mother, a spirit so glorious and radiant that mortal eyes were unable to bear it. Yet this was a sacrifice that would ensure Mama's salvation. For the remainder of her years, Ruth's mother was totally blind—and rapturously content—knowing that her sight would be restored upon entering the Kingdom of Heaven to behold His Paradise.

"You do realize," Abbot Mortimer says to Ruth after she pleads Floyd's case, "that we offer no medical facilities, nor do we have medical practitioners here? Surely he'd be better off in a hospital."

Ruth shakes her head. "Floyd, sadly, is beyond the help of doctors. And then there's all the constant noise, the hustling and bustling everywhere. A hospital is no place for redemption."

"What brought you to our abbey in particular?"

"I believe Floyd would respond well to your approach to Christian instruction. He loves space and stars and what-not. He can always find all the Dippers in the sky."

"Impressive."

"Even more impressive… this place!" Ruth enthuses, sweeping her hands around her. "It's spectacular. I have read nothing but positive things about your Order."

"We have gotten some flattering publicity in recent months," Abbot Mortimer trumpets. He gestures to one of the journal clippings on the wall. "Were you aware we received four crosses in *Divine Places* magazine?"

"Yes, I was. It was how I made up my mind to bring Floyd here."

His vanity massaged, the Abbot manages a smile, but the moment is fleeting.

"I must admit, Miss Greenaway," he says soberly, "while I respect your motives, I have my misgivings. For some, faith is an elusive prospect. Floyd may not have the… capacity for enlightenment."

"Does that mean we deny him the chance?"

"He will not be judged the same as you or I."

"I owe him to try, Father Abbott. I know that with the right attention, he can accept the Lord into his heart and revel in His glory. And that will best prepare him for his journey from this mortal plane into God's heavenly ether."

Abbot Mortimer regards Floyd, who continues to be enthralled by the Solar Christ sculpture.

"Floyd seems a curious young man."

"He is," Ruth attests. "I'm counting on that curiosity to help him see the Light."

The Abbot nods, his decision reached. "Perhaps there is hope for him. He's already quite blessed having you to guide him."

Ruth's eyes brighten. "Then, have you room for us?"

"Our adherent lodgings are presently occupied, but we set aside a few guesthouses for our high-profile devotees. They often show up at their whim. But all these cottages are vacant at the moment, so you may stay in one of them."

"Thank you, Father Abbot. Bless you thousandfold!"

"For as long as you are here, you both must follow our precepts. And should either of you become a burden on the community, or are unable to fulfill your spiritual and manual responsibilities, you will be asked to leave. Understood?"

"Yes. But I promise we won't be any bother."

"Very well then." Abbot Mortimer rubs his hands together and rises from his seat. "Miss Greenaway, it is my great pleasure to officially welcome you and Floyd to the Monastery of the Celestial Christ."

Ruth stands. "This is wonderful! Thank you so much."

She turns to address her companion, still facing away from them gawking at the Solar Christ. "Floyd, did you hear that?"

Floyd doesn't answer.

She steps toward him and taps his shoulder. "Floyd?"

He swivels his body around, a big giddy grin stretched across his face. The head of the sculpture's Jesus figurine is stuck up his nostril.

Ruth gasps and plucks the figure from Floyd's nose. She wipes it on her dress and, frowning sheepishly, gives it to the Abbot.

"Sorry, Father."

"It's quite alright," the Abbot says, unflustered. "I'm sure we'll find a more proper means for our Lord to enter Floyd."

Floyd's head x-rays were already arranged on the lightbox on the wall when Dr. Lieber ushered Ruth inside his office.

After they had wheeled Floyd away on a gurney, Ruth sat for hours in the waiting room of St. Luke's Hospital's emergency department. She'd left her Bible at work, so resorted to reading the arts & crafts magazines available on the end tables. She had just finished an article about how to design a mosaicked birdbath when Dr. Lieber came over and asked her to accompany him.

The doctor sported a royal blue yarmulke and the obligatory white lab coat. His salt-and-pepper beard had a green crumb stuck in it that Ruth at first found distracting, then came to focus on it while they spoke.

With a rollerball pen, Dr. Lieber pointed to a dark blotch on the CT scan image of Floyd's skull.

"This spot here shows a malignant growth in Floyd's ethmoid sinus. That's what caused his nosebleed. It appears to have spread from this area." He circled the tip of his pen around a larger, darker patch covering a sizable portion of the brain. "It's what's called a glioblastoma multiforme, or GBM for short. It's a primary tumor that, unfortunately, is inoperable and, due to its advanced stage, untreatable by radio or chemotherapies."

"You're saying Floyd has cancer?" Ruth asked.

The doctor nodded grimly.

"I'm afraid it's terminal."

"He's—" Ruth's breath caught in her throat. "Floyd's going to die?"

"I'm sorry."

"How long... does he have?"

"Anywhere from one up to possibly six months, depending on the cancer's rate of progression."

For a moment, Ruth had no idea what to say. She'd never before experienced the passing of one of her wards. It was very distressing and somehow disgraceful, as if she herself had failed Floyd.

"Is there no hope, doctor?"

Dr. Lieber stepped toward his desk and sat on the edge of it. He motioned for Ruth to take the chair opposite him. The doctor offered her a box of Kleenex, which she declined.

"We can prescribe a corticosteroid to reduce intracranial pressure. That'll help prevent symptomatic headaches. But you can expect him to exhibit loss of memory or changes in his personality. His being developmentally disabled may either aggravate or mitigate this."

"The poor thing… I don't know what to do."

The doctor asked if Floyd had any relatives she could contact.

Ruth shook her head. "Both his parents were killed in a boating accident years ago. I'm all he has. Just me and the other caregivers."

"How many individuals with special needs do you look after?"

"Seven right now."

"Be aware," Dr. Lieber cautioned, "it's not easy caring for a terminally ill patient in and of itself. It'll be even more challenging when combined with your responsibilities for your other wards. I can recommend a hospice for Floyd. It's more cost effective than staying here, and they can offer the best treatment for someone in his condition, as well as the most comfort."

Ruth regarded him defiantly. "He's most comfortable with us," she said. "We're his family."

———◦———

Brother Guiseppe silently escorts Ruth and Floyd to their accommodations, a tiny hand-hewn timber cottage separate from the main building to provide a semblance of privacy for its typical VIP occupants. Two other monks are already there when they enter, unfolding a roll-away cot in the spartan room. It reminds Ruth of the cabins she stayed in on church retreats as a teenager, except for the slate tile floor, globe lamps, and the circuit board crucifix on the wall with a silver, skyward-staring Christ.

Ruth and Floyd bring in their own luggage. She sets her suitcase down on the floor. Floyd drops his duffel bag with a thud and sits on the regular bed, putting his headphones back on while he takes in his new surroundings.

The two monks finish with the cot and leave, never speaking a word to anyone.

"These will be your living quarters for the duration of your stay," Brother Guiseppe explains to Ruth. "We do not normally lodge two persons in the same chambers, but the Abbot has permitted it in your circumstances."

"And we are very grateful to him for being so accommodating. Aren't we, Floyd?"

Floyd peers out the casement window offering a view of the courtyard garden.

The monk points out the tall, ornate cabinet in the corner. "In the armoire there are your ecclesiastic robes, which are to be worn at all times when outside your cell."

"OK."

"Our morning vigil begins promptly at five-thirty in the church. Attendance for guests is encouraged, though optional. Breakfast is served at six-thirty in the refectory. If you are late, you do not get to eat until lunch at noon. If you are late for that, your next meal is supper at six in the evening. Should you miss that, you are to be without your daily bread."

"That will not be a problem," Ruth assures him.

"As of now, the monastery and its doctrines are your way of life until you depart. Therefore, you are expected to forfeit all cell phones, radios, computers, or any other device that exposes you to the world beyond our walls. Do you have any such items?"

"No sir," Ruth answers.

"What about that?" Brother Guiseppe inquires, referring to Floyd's cassette player.

"That's just his tape player. He likes music. It calms him."

"Be that as it may, to err on the side of caution, I do think I should confiscate it."

The monk reaches toward Floyd to seize the device. Floyd barks "No!" and recoils against the bed's headboard.

"Don't worry," Brother Guiseppe says to him. "It will be returned to you." Again he attempts to take possession of the player, grabbing it by its plastic handle, but is unable to wrest it from Floyd's near-death grip.

"No! No! No!"

"Is this absolutely necessary?" asks Ruth, conflicted between responsibility for her unruly ward and adherence to the abbey's rules. "They're just his silly songs."

Brother Guiseppe, committed to his task, ignores her.

"Young man, don't be difficult. Let it go." Snarling, the monk jerks the player from Floyd's hands. Floyd kicks out his heel, battering Brother Guiseppe squarely in the groin. "Oof!" he exhales and doubles over.

"Floyd!" Ruth thunders.

Floyd snatches his player back and lies on the bed in a fetal position, protectively curling his body around the device.

Ruth cups her palm over her gaping mouth. Brother Guiseppe returns to an erect posture and takes a stiff step backward. He shuts his eyes and inhales deeply, tolerating the pain—*is he reveling in it?*, Ruth wonders—for a few passing moments.

"Are you OK, Brother Giovanni?"

"Yesssssss," he hisses, then composes himself. "And it's Brother *Guiseppe*, miss."

"Yes. Of course. Guiseppe. Sorry."

"All right." The monk glares at Floyd but does not endeavor further to extricate the player from him. "I shall ask the Abbot if he is willing to overlook yet another of our hallowed precepts for you."

"We don't mean to be such a bother."

Brother Guiseppe grumbles, sounding like a little earthquake has triggered in his throat. "Tomorrow after breakfast," he proceeds mechanically, "Prior Weston shall give you a tour of the grounds, as well as familiarize you with our protocols of worship, and provide you with an itinerary of your monastic duties."

Ruth claps her hands together. "My goodness, this is very exciting."

The monk's face remains stoical. "Goodnight, Miss Greenaway."

"Thank you, Brother *Guiseppe*." She smiles. "You've been an excellent host. I'll be sure to compliment you to the Abbot."

The monk nods, then exits.

"Well, this seems cozy enough," Ruth says upon evaluating the room. "What do you think, Floyd?"

"It's very quiet here," he says, still lying on his side in a half-moon.

"Silence is good for the soul. Do you remember what a soul is?"

Floyd shakes his head.

Ruth takes a seat beside him on the bed. "A soul is the most precious thing you have, because God gave it to you. It is your connection to Him. Do you understand?"

Floyd nods blankly.

"It's been a long day, and we have to be up before the crack of dawn. We should get some sleep." Ruth rises and crosses the room to the roll-away. "You can have that bed and I'll take the cot."

Ruth tests the cot's slice-of-bread-thin mattress by pressing her palm down on it. It creaks.

"This will do. Nothing too fancy, but that's not what we're here for, is it?"

Floyd starts snoring.

She tiptoes back to his bed and kneels beside him, clasping her hands in prayer.

"Thank you Lord for lighting my way," she whispers. "And for letting your servants here recognize the promise in Floyd to become a true-hearted believer in You. Amen."

She gently kisses Floyd on his forehead, causing him to stir but not awaken. She switches off the globe lamp on the night table next to him, steeping herself in the brightest darkness she's ever known. For the first time, she believes with all her heart that God has called her, and that she is answering Him.

———⊰✕⊱———

Ruth only broke into tears after she had exited Dr. Lieber's office. As she walked through the hospital halls, she kept her head down to mute her crying. But she needn't have fretted. Even if she were outright bawling at peak decibels she doubted it would disturb anyone around her. Everybody's attention was directed elsewhere—doctors and nurses on their patients, patients on their medical woes, patients' families on each other (or their cell phones).

Ruth found the entrance to the hospital's chapel, a wide white door at the end of a corridor, tucked into its own small wing away from the incessant commotion of the institution. Upon entering, she discovered a simple yet sublime room of worship. It even featured stained-glass windows depicting, due to space limitations, six of the fourteen stations of the cross.

A "Best Of" representation, Ruth concluded.

She took a seat in the empty pew nearest the altar, in front of a shiny brass cross, and began to pray for Floyd. She couldn't beseech God to heal him, could she? The doctor said he was beyond hope, and if taking Floyd was the Lord's will, then His will would be done.

But she had to do *something*. Why would God leave her helpless, powerless, only there to watch Floyd die? It didn't feel right to her.

So Ruth prayed for guidance.

Behind her she heard labored breathing, a half rasp, half whistle. She turned her head toward the brittle, pitiful sound.

Parked in a wheelchair in the left aisle was a person bandaged head-to-toe, mummy-like, wheezing through a small opening over his mouth. Beside him, a chubby black nurse dozed in the pew, producing her own guttural sleep-rattle, a trickle of drool hanging from her bottom lip.

Ruth resumed her prayers, trying hard to tune out the other visitors. Before long, a gaunt middle-aged man in a patient's gown entered, rolling an IV in with him. He sat down in the pew adjacent to Ruth and promptly burst into a fit of wet, hacking coughs, unrelenting thunderclaps that made Ruth's bones tremble.

The serenity of the chapel shattered, Ruth rose and fled, scooping up a saddle-stitched Book of Psalms from a console table on her way out. She returned to Floyd's semi-private room on the third floor. He lay asleep in the adjustable bed closest to the window, which offered a dreary vista of the hospital's rooftop—assorted antennae, turbine vents, and an industrial A/C unit. The other bed was occupied by a liver-spotted elderly man, also snoozing peacefully.

Ruth drew the blue curtain between the beds and pulled up a chair beside Floyd. She opened the booklet she had borrowed to Psalm 34 and read it aloud to him. She'd heard that a person can learn a new language by listening to it in their sleep. Perhaps Floyd might likewise absorb the Word of God. She hoped so. What else could she do?

Then the gunshots started.

Ruth whirled her head toward the torrent of bangs and squealing tires and macho shouting. She flung aside the dividing curtain. The racket blared from a TV installed on the wall in front of Floyd's grizzled suitemate, who was now sitting up in his bed holding the remote. Ruth figured he must have had it up at full volume.

"Sir," she said, raising her voice to compete with the ear-jarring cop show. "Could you please lower your TV?"

The old man didn't respond.

"Sir!"

This time he heard her, saw her, and said, "Huh?"

"Can you lower your TV? It's very loud."

"Sure can," he croaked, smacking his chapped lips. "If you let me squeeze them titties of yours."

Aghast, Ruth huffed and yanked the curtain shut. She banished the odious geezer from her mind and again faced Floyd. He was awake and crying.

"What's wrong, Floyd?"

He sniffled. "I dreamed I was made of air and I could go anywhere I wanted to, and then I tried to go into outer space but I couldn't 'cause there's no air in space and I was sad." He wistfully gazed upwards at the ceiling. "I wanna go up there so bad."

Ruth smiled at him, caressing his head.

"You will, sweetheart," she said.

And he would, she was certain of it, because now she knew what God intended for her to do.

———✳———

Ruth does not sleep well that first night at the Monastery of the Celestial Christ. She dreams of monstrous demons and burning skies and walls dripping with blood. Though these are not the worst dreams she has had lately.

A whimpery, nasally voice ekes into her subconscious. "Rooof."

Ruth opens her eyes. When her vision adjusts to the pale early dawn light that seeps through the window, she realizes Floyd is standing over her. Blood gushes from his nose.

"Mercy," Ruth gasps, jolting upright on her cot. She grabs her pillow, slips the case off, and wads it up, pressing it to Floyd's face.

"Lean your head back and keep your nose covered with this. Hold it there until I say you can take it off, OK?"

He nods, his entire face almost hidden beneath the pillowcase.

"But don't smother yourself!" She springs to her feet, takes his hand, and leads him into their private bathroom.

Floyd doesn't seem all that troubled by his present situation. He sings one of his doo-wop favorites, "Martian

Hop" by the Ran-Dells. Muffled by the pillowcase, it is just barely audible.

Ruth dampens a washcloth with warm water.

"Trade you your pillowcase for this warm towel."

Floyd gives her the crimson-blotched linen. She dabs his nose and lips with the white washcloth, cleaning them off. Blood still oozes from his right nostril. She drapes the cloth over his nose and again tells him to hold it there.

He picks up his song. "We juth dithcovered an important note from thpathe. The Marthianth plan to throw a danthe for all the human rathe." He giggles. "My voith thoundth funny, huh?"

An hour passes before Floyd's nose stops bleeding, long enough for them to miss the morning vigil. They had heard the cue for it playing through the exterior speakers, a shrill vibrato that sounded like somebody slowly deflating balloons. Ruth recognized it from some of the older science fiction movies Floyd enjoyed watching. "Space music" he called it, or rather, with his clogged nose, "thpathe muthic."

They make it to the refectory on time for breakfast. The capacious, high-ceilinged hall is furnished with three long wooden tables with equally long benches on each side of them. Ruth and Floyd wear their ecclesiastic robes, the same as the other two dozen monks there. Floyd complains about the fabric being itchy. The bearded friar sitting next to him jovially says he will get used to it. Floyd responds by mimicking a series of beeps and clicks. The friar has no reply to this.

A trio of monks rolls steel carts out a set of swinging doors. On each cart are trays of food, a steaming medley of scrambled eggs, sausage, beans, and hash browns, as well as pitchers of water and juices. No one begins eating upon being served. Floyd, a forkful of eggs at the ready, whines at Ruth when she grasps his wrist and mouths "not yet" to him. Once their task is done, the servers line up before the rostrum at the far end of the room. One of them strums an autoharp, signaling silence for the recitation of grace.

This is when she first sees him.

He climbs the three steps to the lectern and turns to face the congregation. Ruth is only a couple of seats away from him. He is quite handsome, she thinks. Movie star handsome… no, more than that—beatifically handsome, with his wispy raven hair, frosted blue eyes, and a clean-shaven complexion that, honest to God, glows. His lustrous black robe is emblazoned with the same Star of Bethlehem emblem on its breast as on the Abbot's.

Everybody bows their heads and shuts their eyes. Ruth cannot refrain from sneaking glimpses of him.

His arms outstretched like Christ on the cross, the handsome monk starts to chant in Latin with the heavenliest of voices. Ruth does not understand the language (save for the word "Domine"), but she imagines he is serenading her.

She pictures him approaching her, closer, closer. Her heart quivers as he towers over her, gazing at her with his loving, longing eyes. He takes her hands, coaxes her to rise, and guides her into a tango stance, their bodies joined at the hips. Still singing, he leads her in the sensual ballroom dance, swooping and swirling and swaying together, until his crooning culminates in an "amen" by the congregation.

When Ruth raises her head, she realizes she is still gripping Floyd's wrist. She releases him, saying he can eat now, then sees he already has crumbles of scrambled egg clinging to his lips, chin, and the tip of his nose. He grins at her. She admonishes him and tells him to wipe his face.

After breakfast, Ruth and Floyd file out of the refectory with the other cenobites. They are met by the handsome monk, greeting them with a million-dollar smile.

"Hello, Ruth. I'm Prior Weston. I'll be acquainting you with our way of life here at the monastery."

"Great," Ruth responds, doing her utmost to contain her glee.

"Truth be told, we don't receive many of the fairer sex here. But we're an equal opportunity brotherhood. I, for one, adore a lady who adores the Lord. I find it very… appealing."

Prior Weston's soul-searching eyes linger on Ruth a few moments longer—she is sure she's blushing!—then jump to her ward.

"And this here must be Floyd. Welcome, both of you. Abbot Mortimer has filled me in on your circumstances and may I say, Ruth, your mission is perhaps the most noble undertaking since our own Brother Lucas launched a crate full of the Good Book, with illustrations and recordings, into the farthest reaches of the universe."

"Wow," Ruth says.

"It was a costly enterprise, but who knows what of God's other intelligent life forms may be illuminated by His Word."

"Like Marsians?" Floyd chimes in.

"Martians perhaps. Or Neptunians, Plutonians. Even civilizations beyond our solar system. Imagine, someday we travel to the M81 galaxy and discover little green men quoting the Scriptures. Oh, the possibilities give me goosebumps."

The euphoric Prior shivers. Ruth contracts her own case of goosebumps, though she is envisioning quite something else. She feels warm.

"But I am getting ahead of myself," Prior Weston continues. "If you'll follow me, we shall begin your introduction."

Weston leads them into the grand foyer of the main building, stopping before a tall stone mural—Ruth estimates it must be at least twelve feet high—into which is carved another image of Jesus floating in an outer space vista. For several minutes, the Prior expounds on the Monastery of the Celestial Christ's teachings. Ruth stands beside him, spellbound by his honeyed voice. She is pleasantly surprised to observe that Floyd seems to be listening as well, never once wandering off or crying out or breaking something.

"On the third day," the Prior winds up his oration, "upon rising from the dead, He ascended into heaven, past all the planets and moons and stars of every existing galaxy, where He now sits at the right hand of the Almighty Father. This makes Jesus the very first astronaut. That's why we pay reverence not only to His works here on Earth, but throughout all of God's celestial creations He may touch."

"That is so profound," Ruth says.

"Why aren't we green?" Floyd asks Prior Weston.

"Green?"

Floyd points to the skin of his own arm. "I wanna be green."

"Ahh, I see. God made us in His own image, Floyd. So God is obviously not green, nor blue, nor purple. If He were, we wouldn't be the color we are."

"Marsians are green."

"I've never seen a Martian, so I wouldn't know that. Perhaps it's the light on Mars that makes them look green, but their skin is in actuality just like ours."

"That sounds entirely reasonable, Prior," Ruth says.

"Please. Call me Wes."

"Brother Wes?"

"Just Wes. I'm not a stickler for formalities."

The Prior steps over to a rectangular bronze plaque fastened to the near wall. On it is an embossment of a bald man gazing upward, beneath him the inscription ABBOT RUDOLPH BENNIGAN (1923-1995) and the Psalm verse "By the word of the Lord were the heavens made; and all the host of them by the breath of his mouth."

"Abbot Bennigan was both a devout Christian and a knowledgeable astronomer," relates Prior Weston. "After the moon landing in 1969, he established this monastery as a means of paying spiritual tribute to the wondrous vastness of God's cosmos. He melded old and new approaches to monastic worship." He beams at Ruth proudly. "We like to think of ourselves as St. Benedict meets the Space Age. Some may find that irreverent—"

"Oh no," Ruth reassures him. "I think it's refreshing."

"I agree. I joined this brotherhood because I was not just attracted to its cloistered, contemplative lifestyle, but also to its liberating take on, dare I say it, the stuffy conventions of most other orders. By example, tomorrow you get to attend my afternoon service. We call it our 'Shout and Twist with the Eucharist' mass. A fitting moniker, I do say. I think you'll enjoy it. Everyone does."

"I'm sure we will," Ruth says. "I read all about it in *Divine Places*. I'm really looking forward to it."

The Prior and Ruth lock eyes. There's a connection there, she believes. Something electric between them. She wonders if he feels it too.

Ruth hadn't had many boyfriends growing up, partly because they distracted her from her devotions and partly because they were, according to her mother, "pathways to sin." In grade school she once French kissed Randy Bennett behind the custodial shed, and in trade school she went on a single date with a Christian plumber who turned out to be quite less than Christianly as soon as she got into his truck. That was the sum of her romantic experiences, but she never had very much interest in any boys other than the Lord.

And now, Prior Weston.

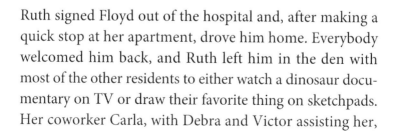

Ruth signed Floyd out of the hospital and, after making a quick stop at her apartment, drove him home. Everybody welcomed him back, and Ruth left him in the den with most of the other residents to either watch a dinosaur documentary on TV or draw their favorite thing on sketchpads. Her coworker Carla, with Debra and Victor assisting her, headed into the kitchen to fix them dinner, a grilled cheese casserole with tomato soup.

Ruth slunk off to Floyd's room. She loaded up a large laundry bag with his clothes and some toiletries. She had already packed a suitcase of her belongings at her place. With everyone preoccupied, she could furtively shepherd Floyd back to her car and be well on their way before anyone was any the wiser.

"What are you doing?"

Ruth looked up to see Carla standing in the doorway.

With the option of sneaking out foiled, Ruth decided to be honest with her, believing she would appreciate the importance of Ruth's mission. She *had* to.

"I'm taking Floyd away."

"What are you talking about?" Carla asked.

"He needs to understand his role in the Lord's design." Ruth stuffed a few rolled-up pairs of Floyd's socks into the sack. "Before he—"

"Stop it, Ruth." Carla stepped into the room and shut the door behind her. "I know you're upset. We all are. But you can't do this."

"I must."

"No, you don't."

"It's what the Lord has directed me to do."

"Really? How did he tell you this?"

"Through Floyd," Ruth answered with conviction.

"So now you're listening to Floyd, are ya? The other day Peter said he ran around the world without stopping. Should I call Guinness Book about that?"

"You wouldn't understand. You don't have faith."

"I have common sense. Always worked for me."

"And I work for the Heavenly Father, Carla. I do His bidding, no questions asked."

"But *I* have questions." Carla crossed her arms. "Like where do you think you're going with Floyd? And for how long?"

"I'm bringing him to a monastic temple for spiritual enlightenment, for as long as required for him to embrace the Holy Spirit."

Carla lowered her voice. "And what if he dies on you on the road?"

"If that happens, then it is God's will. But I must try to help him." Ruth cinched up the laundry bag's drawstring. "I have been called."

"No, Ruth."

"I'll take good care of him, Carla. I promise. There's nothing to worry about."

"You leave here with him and I'm calling the police."

Ruth incredulously considered the woman she has worked alongside the past five years. "Carla—"

"I mean it, Ruth. I am not letting you do this. It's against policy. It's probably kidnapping. And crazy."

"It's not crazy. *I'm* not crazy." Ruth collected herself, clasping her hands together. "One month, Carla," she implored. "Give us just one month. Then I'll bring him back. Please. I need to do this. For his sake. For his soul."

Carla mulled over the proposition. Ruth observed her coworker's—her friend's—expression soften. The Lord had spoken through Ruth, and Carla had listened.

"No. No way." Carla shook her head emphatically. "I love you, Ruth. I really do. But you're crossing the line here professionally. You know that."

Ruth huffed and stamped her foot.

"Can't you see you might hurt Floyd more than help him?" Carla said. "He belongs here, with his friends, with all of us. There's no telling how he'll react if you remove him from his familiar surroundings for a long period of time. He could freak out. And he may be more than you can handle."

"I am capable, Carla."

"You might be. But if not, if shit goes south… hell, even if it don't… you're putting Floyd, yourself, this whole facility at risk. I'm sorry, I can't allow that."

Ruth sighed, resigning herself to what must be done.

"Fine. He'll stay. But I insist on a daily regimen of Christian mentoring."

"I suppose we can arrange something."

"Good. Thank you."

"Thank you, Ruth. You're doing the sensible thing."

Ruth nodded. *But is it the right thing?*, she pondered.

"Now how about comin' to set the table?"

Ruth smiled at her. "Lead the way."

―――◆―――

Wes dominates Ruth's waking thoughts and wildest dreams. He kindles an inferno of untapped desires in her. Lustful feelings yes, but surely not wrong ones. God must have a plan for them.

She looks forward to whatever fruits it would bear!

They'd continued the tour of the monastery grounds, visiting its remarkable chapel, the gardens, the Bennigan Library stocked with Christian and astronomy texts, the famed zero gravity reflection chamber (available for MCC adherent use only), and the gift shop. The Prior gave Ruth a complimentary CD of his newest Christian rock album, *The Lord Is My Rocket.* She bought Floyd a small, hand-crafted glass orb with an etching of Jesus soaring through the heavens.

The three of them had lunch and dinner together. Prior Weston showed an insatiable fascination in Ruth, asking her questions about everything from her family to her faith. And she shared almost everything with him—caring for her ailing mother during her final years, her father deserting them to become a sodomite, even that she was still pure. By nine o'clock, when it is time to retire, Ruth feels closer to him than anyone she has ever known.

To her relief, Floyd hadn't acted out at all, which may count as a minor miracle since she had convinced him to not bring along his cassette player on the tour. Or perhaps something about the Prior—his voice, his personality, his presence—pacified him as much as it excited her. Whatever it had been, she is grateful to Floyd for not intruding on her and Wes's blossoming communion. That night, she reads to him from the Gospel of John the amazing story of Jesus walking on water. After he peacefully dozes off, she too goes to sleep, more content than she has been in ages.

The next day, Ruth and Floyd attend the morning vigil in the chapel. Throughout the entire service she stares up at Prior Weston on the sanctuary. While delivering the homily, he spots her in the congregation and slyly winks at her. Ruth swoons like a fangirl meeting her idol. She supposes she is, but she longs to be so much more.

They eat breakfast afterward—to Ruth's disappointment, Wes is absent from the meal—then perform their assigned duty of dusting the library shelves, a chore Floyd can manage well enough. This is followed by sessions of Bible study, silent contemplation (Ruth lets Floyd listen to his music), and woodworking.

Right after lunch is the event Ruth has been eagerly anticipating all day, Prior Weston's "Shout and Twist with the Eucharist" mass. *Divine Places Magazine* heralded it as "awe-inspiring" and "rapturous" and claimed that it will "make you feel like the blood of Christ Himself is pumping through your veins." Ruth can't wait.

Ruth and Floyd file into the chapel with the rest of the monks. She shuffles down one of the alabaster pews, as near as she can get to the helical truss pulpit, and takes a seat. Floyd slides in beside her, bumping her hip hard.

"Ow, Floyd. Be careful."

Covering the windowless walls of the fantastic chapel are riveted panels of burnished sheet metal, with upside-down pyramid-shaped sconces producing a warm white light. Vertically arrayed on the vaulted ceiling are rainbow-colored neon tubes, blinking in sequence. (These were not on during the morning vigil.) On the altar is a glistening gold cross, and suspended above this is a huge glass-paned sphere with a stained-glass mosaic of Jesus gazing down on the audience.

Though they've been here before, Ruth still marvels at the unorthodox magnificence of the decor. When she first saw it, Ruth thought it was much like Space Mountain at Disney, minus all the heathen tourists.

"I gotta pee," Floyd says to her.

The chapel's lights dim.

"Can you hold it? The service is about to start."

On the opposite side of the rostrum, a scraggly-haired monk begins to play "space music" on a rectangular cherry-wood box with a couple of antennae sticking out of it in different directions. He appears to create its eerie sounds simply by moving his hands in various ways around the antennae, never touching the device.

"I really gotta pee," Floyd reiterates.

"Not now!" Ruth snaps.

Floyd frowns and fidgets his legs.

The overhead speakers emit a resonant drumbeat, evoking a steady pulse that Ruth finds rousing. Then, to her unbridled delight, from a spotlit trapdoor in the center of the rostrum rises Prior Weston, attired in what might be described as Elvis's Amazing Technicolor Dreamcoat, this silver-sequined robe bedazzled with sparkling rhinestones. He also wears wayfarer-style sunglasses like the "Oh, Pretty Woman" singer.

His hands upraised, the Prior yells "Lord, let us rock for Thee!"

The congregation springs to their feet while a power chord blasts from an electric guitar. The firmament-themed iconostasis behind Weston parts like curtains to reveal four monks playing the classic instruments of rock 'n' roll—

guitar, bass, drums, and keyboard—as well as a trio of female backup singers. The band kicks into a hard-driving gospel song Ruth vaguely recognizes. As its frontman Prior Weston belts out the lyrics—"Jesus is just alright with me, Jesus is just alright, OHH YEAH!"—green and blue lasers shoot chaotically from the glass sphere above. Somewhere, a fog machine radiates low-lying mist that billows throughout the chapel.

Weston swaggers up and down the nave with all the charisma of Jesus Christ Superstar. Sometimes he stops and sings a few verses to Ruth.

Awestruck by the immersive audiovisual experience, Ruth is overcome by tingling intoxicating sensations she has never felt. Had she ever been to a rock concert before, she is certain this still would be the best of them all. She yearns to be Wes's biggest fan.

She yearns to be Wes's completely.

The congregation stomps its feet on the floor and pumps its fists in the air.

Tugging insistently on the sash of her robe, Floyd again begs Ruth to use the bathroom.

The Prior's performance and Ruth's ecstasy drown out his pleas.

Many moments later, she realizes Floyd is no longer standing beside her.

The moment after that, in the middle of a reprise of *The Lord Is My Rocket*, the sound and lights in the chapel abruptly cut off.

In one swift motion, Ruth snatched the block-and-tackle nautical lamp from Floyd's bedside table and smashed it across the back of Carla's head. She crumpled to the floor.

Ruth shrunk against the wall, her breath short and her eyes stinging.

What have I done?, she asked herself.

She did what she had to do.

Ruth shut the bedroom door and returned the lamp to the bedside table. She examined Carla's body. Her co-worker was out cold. There were a few drops of blood on the beige Berber carpet near her head. She checked Carla's curly brunette hair. There was a moist, matted clump at the base of her skull, though the area did not seem to be bleeding profusely.

She had no clue when Carla would regain consciousness, so there wasn't any time to dither. Ruth slid her body across the floor to beside the bed, slipped Floyd's pillow underneath her head, and covered her with his blanket.

"Sorry, dear," Ruth said, stroking Carla's cheek. "But God's call trumps all."

Ruth brought Floyd's packed travel bag into the den, setting it down at the threshold of the room. All of the residents were gathered around the TV, some watching it, others diverting themselves by other means—Peter running in place, Lizzie drawing a smiling tree (or possibly Kermit the Frog), Rebecca twiddling her fingers in front of her face.

Ruth crossed the den to where Floyd was sitting on the couch, stooping down to speak into his ear. He shook his head, pointing to the TV screen, now showing a b&w sci-fi flick with alien robots battling human spacetrotters in skintight outfits.

"I wanna finish the movie," Floyd said.

Ruth whispered into his ear again. Floyd grinned, nodded, and stood. She steered him to the entry of the room, then addressed the other residents.

"Everyone. May I have your attention please?"

Only Lizzie looked up at her.

Ruth clapped her hands together twice, prompting most of the others to focus on her, except Peter who kept on jogging in place. Ruth walked over to him and grasped both his wrists, a gesture that instantly slowed him down.

"Stop that, Peter. You'll tucker yourself out."

He froze in place, panting.

"Listen closely everybody," Ruth said. "Laura will be here at six o'clock. That's less than one hour from now. Until then, none of you can leave this room, or else she'll be very, very mad."

"But what if I gotta go potty?" Victor asked. Gregory snickered at this.

"You can leave this room only for that." Ruth punctuated her words by wagging her index finger. "But you must come straight back here after you're done. OK?"

Some nodded. Others repeated "OK."

"What if we get attacked by bears or lions?" asked Debra.

Everybody looked genuinely worried.

"That will not happen. I promise. No bears or lions or any other ferocious animals are allowed in here."

This seemed to mollify them.

"Floyd and I must go away for a while. And if you all pray for him really hard, you'll make him very happy. Right, Floyd?"

"Yeah," Floyd said. "Pray for me!"

"Where are you going, Floyd?" asked Debra.

"It's a surprise!" he answered.

"I wanna surprise too," Gregory said.

The others likewise blurted out their desire for the mystery surprise.

Ruth shushed them. "You'll each get a surprise when Laura gets here, as long as you all stay in this room like we agreed. Right now, it's Floyd's turn for a surprise. So be good ladies and gentlemen, and I know you will all be rewarded."

Ruth smiled at everyone. All appeared quite satisfied with her proposal, some barely able to stifle their enthusiasm. She picked up Floyd's travel bag from the floor, and Floyd went to fetch his Fisher-Price cassette player from the couch. They then bade the others farewell and headed out. Ruth wondered, with a trace of sadness, if she would ever return.

After getting Floyd settled in the passenger's seat and stowing his bag in the trunk alongside her own luggage, Ruth hopped in her car and started the engine.

"Jesus loves you, Floyd," she said. "When you fully understand what that means, you will be ready to join Him in Paradise."

"Is my surprise ice cream? I want ice cream."

"Later," she sighed. "When we're on our way."

———

Ruth, of course, felt remorse for hurting Carla. Such an impulsive, aggressive act was utterly out of character for her. But it could not have been avoided. Hers was a holy mission, decreed by God Himself. And you did not disobey the Lord. He was, above all else, the true boss of her, His policy absolute.

Resolved and renewed in this, her life's purpose, Ruth pulled out from the driveway and onto the road to Floyd's salvation.

"The end of the world is nigh!"

The bright halogen emergency lights had been activated, robbing the chapel of its Space Age spectacle. Abbot Mortimer stands at the pulpit before all Monastery of the Celestial Christ apostles and Ruth. Floyd still hasn't returned. She first thought he had gotten into something, like a fuse box, but that wasn't the case. Weston promised her they'll search for him after the Abbot's announcement.

"We knew this day would come," Abbot Mortimer says. "Abbot Bennigan, the architect of our Order, had prophesied it in 1985, when the Cold War between East and West was thriving. While that tumultuous period had not climaxed in the Armageddon, it did not mean it had been averted. The Book of Revelations foretells fire shall come down from the heavens devastating the Earth, and it appears from all recent media reports that a global war has been initiated. This planet cannot survive our modern weapons and wicked ways.

"Yet we need not perish here, because our brotherhood has readied itself for this eventuality. Today we, along with the sisters of Our Lady of the Empyrean, will journey a great distance toward the constellation of Leo, on a course calculated by our Founding Brothers. From a predetermined point there, our Lord will shepherd us to a hospitable new world He has been reserving for us since the Creation. There we shall build a civilization based on the everlasting tenets of Our God the Father, His Son Jesus Christ, and the Holy Spirit.

"I look forward to taking this trip with you and fulfilling our destiny. I ask you now to please assume your flight operation duties. Brothers, prepare for launch!"

The air crackling with urgency, most everyone hurries off. Ruth remains standing where she is, stunned, confused and lost.

"What do I do now?" she asks herself.

"We possess a large spacecraft," Weston explains to her. "Some rich and powerful allies of ours constructed it for us, as well as the control center underground. They had trained us how to use and maintain everything. We don't advertise this, of course. Most of our highest-profile supporters do not even have knowledge of its existence. It's solely for those who have devoted themselves to our doctrines. Others might view it as... eccentric perhaps, equating us to some state-of-the-art cult."

"I understand. The Lord's work must endure."

"Yes, Ruth. And it will. And that is something I need to discuss with you." He puts his perfectly manicured hand on her shoulder. "You are here when momentous events have precipitated us to embark on establishing our new settlement. I don't believe it is mere happenstance."

"No? What is it?"

"I believe the Lord wants you to join us."

"You mean… up there?" Ruth lifts her eyebrows. "In space?"

"All the universe is God's creation. We will be living according to the same principles, but on a different one of His worlds."

"But how do you know this different world exists?"

"Over the years we've done an enormous amount of mathematical computations and astronomical surveys employing the most advanced technology. We already have a good idea where this planet is located. And most importantly, we have faith."

"It sounds so… scary."

"It is. And you are free to choose not to go. Though that would be a fatal choice."

"There must be others more deserving. I imagine seating is limited."

"The sisters at Our Lady of the Empyrean just down the road will play an integral part in repopulating the new world. Nineteen of them are capable of bearing children. Twenty-seven of our brothers are going. That's forty-six people. The ship holds fifty-two. So we have room for you. But you must decide quickly."

Ruth's heart races. "This is all so overwhelming. How can one decide something like this?"

Weston takes her hands, pressing them to his bosom. "I know you have feelings for me, Ruth. I confess, I feel them for you too. If I may be blunt, I'm highly attracted to you. The chemistry we have, it's undeniable. Ordained. I'd be honored to have you as my partner in the new world. There is no future for us on this one."

Everything Wes says makes sense, Ruth thinks. There *is* a reason she is here, now, with him. It was fated to be.

Her fear is reasonable too. Yet if she is to uphold her mission, she must have faith as well. And she has to admit, the thought of laying with Wes excites her.

"OK," Ruth says, resolute. "Let's go."

The Prior beams. "Splendid!"

"I'll share the blessed news with Floyd when we find him. He'll be beyond thrilled to be going into space."

The Prior furrows his brow. "I'm sorry, Ruth. Floyd cannot come."

"Pardon me?"

"Floyd can't come with us."

"Why not? He's the reason why I came here."

"I understand that, and I know you must be feeling an obligation to him. But he would not contribute anything of value to our colony. In fact, he would taint our gene pool should he even reproduce."

Thrown for a curve, Ruth rallies to defend her ward.

"It's not Floyd's fault he was born the way he is. He's still one of God's children, is he not?"

"Yes, he is. But there's no place for him where we're going, no part for him in what we need to do. You can see that, Ruth, can't you?"

"My mission was—is—to save Floyd. What will become of him without me?"

"He'll be transported to one of our nearby properties by someone who has elected to remain behind. We own a beautiful lakefront resort where there's no light pollution. Floyd will be able to see all the stars in the sky tonight. Not a bad way to spend what may be his last hours on Earth."

"I can't just abandon him."

"You're not, Ruth. He will be cared for."

"This is…" Ruth rakes her fingers over her eyes and down her cheeks. "Horrible."

"It really isn't though. Think practical. Armageddon aside, Floyd doesn't have long to live anyway. Why would you deny yourself the chance to survive?"

"My life's purpose," she mutters.

"What did you say?"

"I am not going, Prior," she says louder, adamantly. "Floyd needs me now more than ever."

"Ruth, I beg you, please reconsider—"

"I already have. I'm his caregiver. I'm responsible for him. Mine will be the last voice he hears, and God's the last words."

The Prior nods, with a slightly crestfallen smile that almost breaks Ruth's heart.

Not exactly mission accomplished, she concedes to herself. Yet she can live with it, however briefly that may be.

———◦———

When Ruth and Floyd, toting their baggage, reach Ruth's car in the monastery parking lot, two gray passenger vans have arrived. Riding in them are a group of young women in midnight blue habits. The sisters from Our Lady of the Empyrean, Ruth presumes. They step off the vehicles and enter the building. Ruth fleetingly wonders which one of them will become Wes's partner on the new world.

The monks had tracked down Floyd in their kitchen pantry, polishing off a box of Fig Newtons. Floyd apologized to everyone he saw, believing he was in big trouble. Ruth told him it was fine, that he was forgiven. She never knew he liked Fig Newtons.

Ruth drives them twenty-three minutes away from the monastery before stopping at a service plaza off the expressway. There were already long lines at the pumps for gas. It took almost half an hour for her to fill up the Kia. She didn't mind though. She wasn't in a rush to get anywhere. She wasn't sure yet where to go.

Prior Weston had offered her and Floyd access to the brotherhood's lake resort, but that feels a bit awkward to her, an unearned consolation. She's always wanted to visit the Grand Canyon and the Rocky Mountains, but they are too far away.

Floyd asks if they are going home. Ruth ultimately agrees to this. She will willingly suffer whatever the consequences may be for her crimes, and Floyd will be with his friends at the end. This seems the right thing to do all around.

They head inside the convenience store to buy snacks and drinks. Three other customers and the pimply clerk watch the TV mounted above the counter. It's a local newscast reporting on the current grim state of affairs.

Various cities along the West Coast have been struck by intercontinental missiles, massive explosions have destroyed swaths of New York, Boston, and Washington D.C., and the full brunt of the nation's Armed Forces have been deployed to counter hostilities here and abroad. All over the world, people are praying, panicking, and pummeling each other.

"Shit's goin' down," one man in a forest camo jacket says as he bolts out the door. The other two customers start stocking up on as much foodstuffs, beverages, and medical supplies as they can carry.

On the way back to the car with their Xpress Mart bags, Ruth spots a slim fiery object soaring across the blue sky, a dense plume of smoke trailing it. Ruth reckons it could be the brothers and sisters fleeing the Earth in their spacecraft. She hopes they will find the paradise they seek. She hopes everyone does.

"Look, Floyd." Ruth points. "A rocketship."

"Wow." He gapes at it.

She leads him over to a picnic table. They sit down. She gives him a plastic spoon, keeping one for herself, then passes him one of the two chocolate ice cream cups. She considers reading to him from the Bible while they eat, but instead lets him listen to his cassette player. She leaves the book in her handbag.

Together they watch the rocket travel overhead.

"I'm gonna go up there someday," Floyd says.

"That'll be nice, Floyd," answers Ruth.

He cannot hear her over his music.

THE BEHOLDER

This morning, one much like most other mornings, Alex awakens beneath the shuttered factory's awning of corrugated steel. He yawns and stretches and wipes the crust from his eyes. His bladder ready to burst, he scampers for the condemned apartment house nearby and makes his way to its summit by scaling the rusted ironwork of the fire escape.

At the ledge he peers across the rooftops at the sun rising over his city, a sight that never fails to rouse him. He then unzips the fly of his baggy, ragged cargo pants and lets the warm golden fluid flow from him. He watches it cascade in a gentle arc, meeting the ground three floors below. The stream spatters on the cracked concrete, the droplets sparkling in the dawn light.

As the last of it dribbles from him, Alex stares down at his creation and smiles. Another glorious new day has begun for him. Again he blessed the world with something good, something beautiful. Something he made himself. He is the source of this beauty, and for that he is proud.

Alex climbs down and kneels over the frothy pool. He gazes into it, the bubbles reflecting the gleam in his eyes. Thoroughly contented, he ventures out, his hunger leading him.

Pressing his ear up against the glass of the electronics store, Alex hears the news man on the television set in the window say it is Sunday. This makes Alex happy. Saturdays are when his favorite restaurant is the most crowded, often fully booked for dinner. He knows there will be plenty for him today.

Many evenings Alex has spent sitting patiently on the corner across from the eatery, waiting to catch a glimpse inside it when its bronze double doors opened. On these occasions, he has seen a wondrous jungle of potted plants within… handsome waiters in crisp black blazers racing back and forth with round silver trays on their shoulders… suspended brass lamps glowing and flickering like candle flames… sweeping gilt-framed paintings of whaling ships and fishing trawlers hanging on the dusky walls.

Alex slinks around to the rear of the restaurant and lifts the heavy metal lid to its mammoth dumpster. Digging meticulously through the debris, he uncovers a feast of steak morsels, bits of lobster, partially eaten buttered sweet rolls, and slivers of rich chocolate cake. He devours these delicacies and, when his belly is sated, embarks on his afternoon stroll around the city.

Alex marvels at the skyscrapers towering over him with un-rivaled dignity. Flocks of pigeons swoop and soar balletically above him. People mill around him heedlessly. Alex drifts among them, stirred by the rhythm of their spirited chatter, the honking of crosstown traffic, the rumbling of construction work, and the melodies of street musicians playing for coins and applause.

The pulsing beat titillates Alex's ears. He dances to it, twirling gracefully, laughing. All the smells, pungent blends of fragrances and stenches, tickle his nostrils. He strokes the smooth branches of saplings lining the curbs, plucks their green waxy leaves, kissing them with his dry, chapped lips—oh, there is the falafel man with his blue baseball cap, pushing his hot cart! Alex greets him with the friendliest of smiles and a cheery "hee-lo Fella Full Man!"

Alex yearns to pet a puffy poodle dog, but its master tugs hard on its leash, hurrying off when Alex draws too close.

He plays with a cockroach, blowing on it to make it scurry about in different directions, then lets it go free into a sewer drain.

A police man taps the soles of his bare calloused feet with a club while he naps in a vestibule, urging him to move on.

He quenches his thirst with tepid cola from a half-empty bottle left at the base of a streetlamp.

Some children spit on him then run away, giggling and shouting bad words.

He whistles a jaunty tune that lingers in the haze of his memory.

As he tires from his daily wanderings, Alex realizes the sun is setting, painting the clouds a bright shimmery orange. Nibbling on a piece of stale pretzel he had found in a gutter, he seeks out a place to sleep.

He soon comes upon a little tailor shop downtown, its window displaying long coats draped on faceless mannequins. Over the entrance is a weather-battered sign with chipped yellow lettering Alex cannot read.

He circles around the building into a deserted alley strewn with cigarette butts, fast food bags, and beer cans. Twine-bound bundles of frayed fabric lie along the brick wall. Alex judges this a cozy enough bedding for a night's rest. He mounts the bundles and crawls into the center of the heap. He tears off some of the soft material and wraps himself in it to protect him from the chill of the night.

Once he's comfortably tucked in, Alex pulls from his waistband a crushed cigar he has been saving and smokes it. He farts and coughs and picks crumbs from his bushy black beard. He then shuts his weary eyes, sighs approvingly, and dozes off…

Alex is startled awake by panicked, pleading cries. Cowering underneath his makeshift blanket, he peeks through a gap between a pair of aluminum trashcans.

Before him in the dim alley stands a gray-haired man in a gray business suit, his eyes wide, his breath quick, his chest heaving. Behind him, a tall teenaged boy cups one hand over the man's mouth and thrusts a switchblade to his throat with the other. He whispers into the man's ear. The man nods. The boy cautiously releases his clasp on the man's mouth and, still gripping the knife against his jugular, explores the man's loose pockets.

The man grabs the boy's forearm, struggling to pull it away from his neck. The blade slices his chin. He forces himself out of the boy's hold and stumbles away from him.

The boy lunges, stabbing the man deep in the throat. He collapses, hands clutching his gushing neck. The boy fumbles through the man's pockets and removes a bulky wallet, then dashes into the night.

It begins drizzling. A loud howling siren gets closer. Alex flees the alley until the sound of the siren has faded in the distance.

At ease once more, he saunters up the flashing-neon city blocks. The wet pavement glistens. Steam billows from manholes. Cool raindrops run down his cheeks.

Alex never before witnessed a man die. He's mesmerized by it… the way the man's body buckled, his face white and frozen like a statue… the way his blood spouted from the gash, a dark halo forming beneath his head… the way his gargled groans echoed off the alley walls, a floating euphony. It is one of the most beautiful things Alex has ever beheld. Even better than a puddle of his piss twinkling in the sunshine.

Alex rolls the switchblade's red handle in his palm. In his haste, the boy had dropped it. It slid next to where Alex hid. As soon as the boy was out of sight, Alex scooped up the knife and slipped it into his pocket.

It's smooth and slender, like a pencil or paintbrush.

Come the morning, the streets refill with people. Alex sees potential in them all. He spots the falafel man in the blue baseball cap parking his hot cart on a corner. Gripping the blade, Alex walks toward him, smiling, eager, inspired. Ready to create something beautiful.

MR. GREGORI

Mr. Gregori was already there when Emma moved into her new apartment.

She'd fallen in love with the early twentieth century greystone the instant she saw it. It was only five subway stops away from her paralegal job, and the eastside neighborhood was charming and affordable enough for her. The two-bedroom was not as large as she had desired, but it was cozy, with a walk-in closet, a washer/dryer, and a recently renovated kitchen. A week later she signed the lease, had her furniture brought over, and called it home.

It was Mr. Gregori's home too. Had been since 1954. In '57 he mistakenly conjured the wrong demon to help with his struggling Italian restaurant. The monstrous beast, named Aka Manah, turned out to be from one of the higher echelons of Hell. Angry at having been summoned by such a lowly mortal, it made Mr. Gregori immortal—and the mirror image of itself. Still attired in the white slub weave shirt and brown flannel trousers he wore for the botched invocation, Gregori had become a nightmarish parody of a

Sears-Roebuck ad. He'd been a handsome man once. Now he chilled himself every time he caught a glimpse of his own hideous reflection.

The demon's curse produced three additional effects: Gregori could not leave the apartment, he was incorporeal, and he was invisible to others. Each of these posed pros and cons. Being trapped anywhere for eternity was misery, but at least it was in a place where he felt comfortable. Being tantamount to a ghost meant he couldn't pick up any objects, but he could walk through walls and never stub his toe. Being invisible meant nobody would be terrified by his inhuman appearance, but it also lent to him feeling awfully lonely despite the company of all those who had taken up occupancy there since he'd gone missing and the landlord declared his apartment abandoned.

Mr. Gregori's cohabitants over the years had been a sundry lot. A Jewish family of seven inhabiting an area that had narrowly sufficed for him alone. A middle-aged man who collected antique dolls. An old lady who painted only barren desert landscapes. A gay couple who had staggering amounts of sex. A straight couple who had no sex at all, at least not with each other. Decades of different tenants sharing Mr. Gregori's home without them ever knowing he was there. Save for a fleeting curiosity, he felt nothing for them.

Then came Emma. The moment he laid eyes on her, Gregori swore she would never leave.

He wouldn't let her.

Emma adored her new third-floor apartment. All her furniture fit where she wanted it, there was plenty of storage space, and the art nouveau-styled front window offered a magnificent view of the uptown city skyline.

The only thing she didn't like was the drafts.

For the life of her, Emma could not figure out where the ice-cold puffs of air were coming from. They did not happen all the time, nor always in the same spots. It was maddening. She would be sitting on her sofa, or in her bed, or at the dining table, then feel a sudden chill on her bare arms, cheeks, and neck. And the drafts followed a rhythm, starting and stopping for equal durations.

Like someone was breathing on her.

"I'm at my wit's end," Emma said to her sister on the phone.

"It has to be coming from *somewhere*, Em. Unless you're just imagining it."

"I'm not imagining it, Dee."

"Remember when mom and dad took us camping in the Adirondacks and you thought there were ants crawling all over you?"

"It's *not* the same."

Emma didn't blame her older sister for being skeptical. As a child, Emma had been prone to fantasizing about mythical worlds, fabled creatures, and yes, the occasional molestation by illusory insects. Dee, in contrast, had been solidly rooted in reality, never engaging in make-believe play. It was ironic then that Emma wound up in the law field, while Dee became a Lutheran minister. Theirs wasn't an especially religious family—they had been "holiday Christians" for the better part of Emma's upbringing—but Dee believed the Father, Son, and Holy Spirit had called her. Emma still had a difficult time visualizing her sister praising God and saving souls for a living, but she was proud of her regardless.

"I'm not crazy."

"I didn't say you were," Dee replied.

"My landlord doesn't have a clue what's up. Tells me he re-insulated the walls and installed energy-efficient windows, so there shouldn't be any drafts. He couldn't find any when he checked."

"So what are you gonna do?"

Emma sighed, mulling it over.

"You could come spend the night here, see for yourself that it's real."

"What good will that do?"

"I'll have somebody to back me up when I talk to my landlord again. And maybe you can pinpoint where it's coming from."

"If you couldn't, what makes you think I'll be able to?"

"Please Dee. I need your help."

Dee acquiesced. They made plans for her to stay over Friday night and do brunch at the Olive Café on Saturday, Emma's treat. When she hung up the phone, Emma felt a little better.

She felt less scared.

Gregori observed Emma with swelling, insatiable ardor. Each day he'd discovered something new about her that attracted and aroused him. These were strange yet welcome experiences for him, ones he had forgotten ages ago but now returned like a fresh breeze in a stuffy room.

He had never married, as he was too busy laboring to keep his restaurant afloat. Yet he was no flop with the ladies. Prior to the curse, his striking looks, natty dress, and unwavering charisma grabbed the eye-batting attentions of many of the city's most attractive women. Sometimes he would indulge them. But they were largely disposable things that seldom held his interest for long.

None of them compared to Emma—her porcelain doll face, ringleted golden hair, and moss green eyes seduced him.

She walked with light, graceful steps, as if dancing some silent ballet. Her laugh was beautiful, buoyant music to his ears. Her voice sang even when she spoke, never turning raspy or shrill no matter her mood.

She dressed fashionably, modestly, which made her act of undressing, unveiling her flawlessly sculpted body, all the more exciting for him to see unseen. He drank in all of her, savoring every curve and cleft.

She was a goddess, an angel, a divine vision.

He yearned to be close to her.

Closer…

But damned as he was, Gregori could never touch her, talk to her, tell her how much he loved her. And she would never be able to love him, nor even acknowledge his presence.

It was the worst anguish he had yet endured.

Emma often sensed she was being watched. This feeling accompanied the drafts—*the breathing*. It unnerved her.

She entertained the idea that her apartment might be haunted, like the Doherty family's bed & breakfast in her hometown. As a child, Emma had played throughout the historic house with their daughter Lily. Sometimes they saw hazy gray apparitions roaming the upstairs hall at dusk. They later learned the dwelling had once operated as an infirmary during the Civil War, where many soldiers had perished from their wounds.

Emma's current landlord, however, insisted that no deaths, tragic or otherwise, ever occurred in her building. Old editions of the city newspaper she'd pored through at the library supported this. Miss Creighton, who had lived on the street for sixty-six years, told her the most terrible thing she remembered was when eight-year-old Wallace Becker three doors down used a blanket to parachute off the roof and broke near every bone in his body.

Nevertheless, sometimes Emma would say out loud in her apartment, "Who's there?" There was no answer, of course. She knew she was being silly.

She hoped her sister would fix the draft problem, or at least ease her mind about it. She also considered asking Dee to bless her place. It couldn't hurt.

So Emma *was* aware of him! Why else would she ask who was there when nobody else but he was around?

As elated as Mr. Gregori was by this revelation, he wasn't certain what it could mean.

Could he somehow breach the confines of his curse? Was there a way to reach her, to be with her, as lovers fated and true?

He pondered this. He could try reciting the same invocation that had resulted in his plight, hope he would not require the ritual accoutrements—the chalk pentagram, the black candles, his blood—and, if successful, persuade the demon to restore his flesh, even if he must surrender his very soul this time.

Then he remembered how grotesque he was. That rancorous demon would not be so obliging to change him back into his handsome prior self, and the curse would only be made much more grievous if he were to again become corporeal. No doubt Emma would be horrified by the sight of him. She would never love a monster.

Still, if he could physically manifest himself, Gregori could fulfill other yearnings he had.

If he must be a monster, he would behave like one.

After they had gone out to dinner at the Mediterranean bistro on Addler Avenue, Emma's sister inspected every window, door frame, and wall fixture in her apartment.

Nothing could account for the drafts.

"Maybe I *was* just imagining it," Emma said, resigned to never resolving the mystery.

"I'm not a professional repairman, so don't take what I say as Gospel."

"Ha."

Her sister had a knack for cheering her up, as well as for championing her. In grammar school, when another girl pushed Emma into the mud, Dee mocked the bully's frizzy ginger hair until she cried. In middle school, she'd made a boy eat a millipede after he put his gum in Emma's ponytail. In high school, she used a Chemistry textbook to break the nose of a boy who called Emma a slut, earning herself a month suspension. That's how it always was. Dee stood up for her, fought for her, protected her.

Since becoming a woman of the cloth, she still looked out for her, albeit in a more saintly style, dispensing advice both practical and spiritual. While Emma may never get used to the clerical collar she wore, Dee was the same big sister she knew and trusted and loved.

"If it keeps bothering you, you can always move out."

Emma huffed. "I just moved in."

Dee sat down on the sofa beside her. "So what do you want to do, Em?"

"We can watch *The Exorcist*."

"That's not really my type of movie."

"Oh." Emma arched her eyebrow. "I'd thought you guys would be quoting it all the time, like Monty Python."

"Not when the demon has the best dialogue."

Emma chuckled. "How about *Monsters, Inc.*?"

"Sure. Got any popcorn?"

Emma nodded. "Second shelf in the pantry."

"I'll pop. You cue up the movie."

Dee headed off into the kitchen. Emma plucked the DVD from the rack and loaded it into the player.

The ritual failed this time. Maybe he did need all the bells and whistles. Maybe he spoke the words wrong. The tatty grimoire he'd originally consulted—acquired from a self-professed warlock running an occult store on West Ninth Street—was long gone from the apartment (not that he could grip it if it weren't), and his memory of the invocation may well be faulty. Whatever the reason, no demon materialized. No deals could be struck. Mr. Gregori was stuck as he was.

He was as close to Emma as he would ever be.

It was not nearly close enough.

Emma's sister arrived. Gregori, too out of temper to be an invisible spectator, cloistered himself in the walk-in closet. He wanted to rip the clothes off the hangers, yank down the shelves, stomp on the boxes, punch holes in the walls. Anything to vent his frustration and fury. But he could do nothing. He couldn't even hear himself roar from rage.

So he mutely wept, a wretched unloved thing.

After a while, Mr. Gregori peeked through the closet door. He could see Emma seated on the sofa, reading a magazine. Her stout, snorty sister had left the room.

Emma looked so lovely, so luminous. So alone.

He wished he could make her smile, laugh, bring her to ecstasy. She had never brought a lover home with her—how harrowing that would have been for Mr. Gregori! He'd often fantasized about being with her, in her.

In her.

He knew it wouldn't be like the real thing, but perhaps it would gratify him more than his purely voyeuristic acts. He shuffled up to Emma. He hovered his clawed hand over her breast, then slid it through her sweater, through her skin, and into her heart. He watched her shiver. She draped a quilt around herself.

Gregori's mind blazed with rekindled passions.

He leaned toward her, opening his misshapen maw and wiggling out his black, wormish tongue. He inserted it between her slightly parted lips in a pretense of a lovers' kiss. He then merged his face with Emma's, licking the inside of her skull, lapping at her brain, and slipping down her throat…

———◦———

Dee shook the Jiffy Pop pan on the gas burner until its foil cover was fully inflated and the popping nearly stopped. She removed it from the stove and gingerly sliced the foil open with a steak knife, releasing a billow of steam.

The smell of the popcorn evoked memories of when their mother had made it for her and her little sister. Those were happy times, innocent times, before Dee recognized true evil in the world. The Lord, of course, inspired her in her works, but it was the guileful influence of the Devil on God's children that compelled Dee to become a minister. Though she supposed she had always displayed a natural propensity for defending the vulnerable.

She thought about growing up with Emma. Her sister had been a delicate, whimsical child, believing in fairies and unicorns and mermaids to the degree where she would cry buckets if anyone told her they were not real. While Emma ceased believing in them long ago, by her teenage years she began exhibiting more disturbing delusions— shadowy figures following her around or standing outside her window, above her bed, watching her. A psychiatrist had prescribed medications to curb these frightening sensations, and Emma had been seemingly fine for the past ten years.

And now this breathing business.

Dee worried that her sister had gone off her meds. When she asked her if she were still taking them, Emma acted offended. She insisted, over and over, that her mind was not playing tricks on her. But she wouldn't answer Dee's question.

Dee poured the popcorn into a bowl and sprinkled salt on it. In spite of the circumstances, she was glad to be spending this time with her sister. It almost felt like they were kids again, to be sitting in front of the TV, gossiping and giggling and being goofballs together. Maybe that's what Emma really needed, to feel carefree for a while, without any shadows in her world.

Heartened, Dee headed back into the den.

"What in Hell?!"

Gregori withdrew from Emma and whirled toward the shrieking voice. Her pious sister stood at the threshold of the room, mouth agape, eyes drawn in shock.

The God-glorifying skag could see him!

"What's wrong?" Emma yelled.

"Get away from her!"

Her sister dropped the bowl of popcorn she held and snatched the bronze statuette of praying hands from the credenza. She charged at the monster. On reflex, Gregori flinched, but didn't dodge the oncoming bludgeon. He did not fear injury for he could not be hurt.

The statuette struck his shoulder, sending ripples of intense pain, of recalled agonies through him. His nerves ignited like fuses, bursting like fireworks. The blow stunned him, stirring him as spectacularly as any orgasm he could dream of having.

Oh, you sweet angel. She made him feel something!

Emma's sister raised the statuette again to smite the infernal creature. Gregori regained his wits and went on the offensive. He leapt at his attacker, sinking his jagged fangs into her neck. She gagged as Gregori rent flesh and muscle like a ravenous wild beast.

Emma screamed.

Mr. Gregori tasted blood. It tasted exquisite.

Emma never returned to the apartment after that night. She had been, quite reasonably, the prime suspect in her sister's death. Her assertion that Dee's throat just ruptured itself was of course met with much skepticism by the investigating detectives. Yet, they could never account for how she had received the wounds, which the autopsy concluded were characteristic of some large animal bite. There was no foreign blood or saliva; no weapon was found that explained it. Without corroborating evidence of her guilt, Emma was released. She relocated to Pittsburgh to reside with her mother.

The case remains unsolved.

Nobody wanted to live in the third-floor apartment. Within months, the other tenants in the building also left. As it'd proved difficult to lease any of the apartments for their fair market value, the owner chose to sell the property to a restaurateur, who converted the space into an upscale bar and grill named DARK. The gruesome death that had taken place on the premises only seemed to attract more customers. The establishment has become a stop on many ghost tours in the city.

The interior is appropriately dim, with walnut woods, brick walls, and oil lamps. Zagat's gave it a respectable 22 rating. The service is excellent and the menu on par for a restaurant of its caliber, touted for its marinated ribeye, crusted halibut, and glazed lamb shank.

The entire third floor is a roomy cocktail lounge with clusters of high top tables set with votive candles. It's an appealingly ambient venue for couples and businesspeople, one presenting only a single drawback.

Despite their best efforts, the proprietors never could eliminate the odd-occurring drafts some patrons likened to cold, quiet breaths.

FYVP

Steve climbs the subway stairs, emerging from the deserted bowels of the city into its dark, dirty asshole. Closed for hours, the shells of auto body shops, secondhand appliance dealers, and ghetto churches line the block. The footsteps of his Doc Martens echo off their weathered brick facades. Towering streetlamps hazily illuminate the pavement, still wet from an earlier rainfall. Rats and roaches fearlessly scavenge cracks and crevices. Used condoms and needles litter the gutters, graffiti and puke spray the walls.

Downtown, a haven for the lost and the hiding.

Over the past six months, Steve has become a proud connoisseur of body modification. He pierced three holes in each lobe, strung dangling chains from them linked to the gold bone plugged through his nose. His forehead is dotted with chrome-plated studs. Kaiser spikes jut out from his eyebrows. Bull's rings punch through his nipples. He had treated himself to seven lip hoops and a tongue barbell for Christmas, making the holiday uncommonly joyous for him.

And tonight, just picturing that ribbed loop inserted through the glans of his cock excites him beyond reason. He fantasizes about hanging tackle weights from it, stretching it to the brink of breaking.

Steve is heavily tattooed with vivid images of death and damnation, a gallery he had begun a decade ago when attending community college in the 'burbs, but that sort of shallow decoration does nothing for him anymore. He wants to push his flesh to its limits, not just mark it.

He supposes he's a masochist, though he doesn't like leather whips or hot wax or even clover clamps. He *needs* to feel the ecstasy of pronged metal puncturing his skin, sliding through meat and muscle.

Yeah, it's way better than fucking, he thinks. And he has to admit, he likes the attention, be it from the shocked old fogey on her way to her bingo game or the rocker chick with a taste for the weird and wild. He loves any looks he gets, because he hates not being noticed. Can't stand being ignored.

By now he figures he is pretty impossible to ignore. But that doesn't stop him from adding more shiny embellishments to himself. He's hooked.

Steve learned about *FYVP* from a flyer handed to him by a stunning platinum blonde at the Volcano Club where he bartends. She told him they specialize in exotic cosmetic piercings at affordable prices, no appointment necessary. And, being open until four in the morning, it fit Steve's after-hours lifestyle.

He fishes the flyer from his back pocket to recheck the address. One block down, on Carver Street.

The parlor is housed on the ground level of a squat five-story tenement, identified only by a small plastic sign designating its name and business hours. He almost walks by the entrance.

Sporting a black T-shirt and leather pants adorned with superfluous zippers, Steve steps into the sparsely furnished lobby. A half dozen empty folding chairs are set along the pastel-colored walls. A slim young receptionist with too much mascara, her raven hair tied up in a bun, sits at a desk, focused on filing her purple lacquered nails with an emery board.

Steve gives the area the once-over and, with a nod of approval, swaggers up to the girl.

He fake-coughs to get her attention.

The girl raises her eyes from her manicure. "May I help you?"

"Yeah," he answers, feeling more awkward than he expected himself to be. "I'm here to get my penis pierced."

"Are you alone?"

"Yeah," he smirks. "Just me and my weenie."

"Through there," she directs Steve with a gesture of her thumb. "End of hall. Mister Holland will service you."

"Thanks, babe." He winks at her. She blows the dust off her fingernails.

Steve slips through a Bali bead curtain and advances down the long, narrow corridor. A naked light bulb on the ceiling flickers, its harsh glow casting his blurry reflection on the glossy wood paneling.

At the end of the corridor, he reaches the threshold of a spacious white room, antiseptically bright. In the center of the room is a vinyl-upholstered table, bolted to the floor, about the size of a twin bed. Maroon drapes cover a substantial portion of the far wall. In one corner is a tall metal cabinet with several shallow drawers.

Hunched at the cabinet rummaging in a drawer, Steve presumes, is Mister Holland, tall and lean. He turns toward his customer with a toothy grin.

"Hello, sir! Welcome to *FYVP*," he greets Steve in a hotel-hospitality tone. "Come on in."

Mister Holland wears brown suede shoes, expensive ones, and beige pants and white buttoned shirt, the sleeves rolled up above his elbows. He has a permanently furrowed brow above wire-rimmed glasses. He is older than Steve had anticipated, well into his fifties, his dark hair streaked with gray.

"Hey. I'm interested in a Prince Albert."

"I know! Marybee has already informed me."

Steve guesses Marybee is the receptionist's name. He will use it after he's done here to strike up a conversation with her. Maybe Marybee can be the first to try out his new tricked-out dick.

"Please. Lie down on the table."

Steve hoists himself up onto the table while Holland shuts the heavy door to the hallway.

"Were you aware the Prince Albert piercing had been named after Queen Victoria's husband and consort Prince Albert of Saxe-Coburg and Gotha? He invented it in order to subdue the appearance of his well-endowed penis in tight trousers. At least, so says the urban legend."

"Cool," Steve replies, casually adjusting himself.

"All rightee. Please put your arms at your sides."

"You take credit cards, don't ya?"

"Indeed we do. Now, arms at your sides."

Steve thrusts his fists to his thighs. "Shouldn't I take my pants off, or whip it out?"

"No need," Mister Holland says as he fastens one of Steve's wrists taut to the table with a looped thong, pulls a connecting tether across his midsection, then binds down his other wrist.

"What ya doin'?"

"Just relax, sir," Holland reassures him. "It's only a precaution. Some people, as a reflex, try to knock my hand away as soon as I puncture the skin." He chuckles, circling Steve. "We don't want to make this any more difficult than necessary."

Makes sense, Steve supposes.

Mister Holland then, more forcibly, straps his ankles down.

"What the hell, man?" Steve squeals. "Is this really… I mean, I can handle it. You don't have to tie me up like this."

"It's part of the ritual."

Steve scoffs. "What ritual?"

"Preparing you," Holland informs him as he lastly, roughly, straps Steve's head down so he can hardly move it.

"For what?" Steve barks.

"To be a star!"

"Get these fucking things off me!" Steve yells, his every muscle rigid from anger and alarm.

———

163

Mister Holland ignores him, tearing off his T-shirt with the quick snip of a scissor. He then rotates the table, tilting it upward at a sixty-degree angle. Steve, now facing the drapes, watches Mister Holland flip a switch by them. There is an amplified pop, followed by the faint hum of feedback. He then tugs a cord next to the curtain. It parts to reveal an enormous window. Beyond it is a company of elegantly dressed people, middle-aged men and women, some seated at a counter at the window, others standing behind them. Everybody holds a flute of champagne. All gaze at Steve.

"Can you all hear me alright?" Holland bellows.

The crowd whoops in affirmation.

"Excellent! Without further ado," Mister Holland announces, displaying all the zeal of a ringmaster, "it's showtime, folks!"

The audience cheers.

"Tonight, ladies and gentlemen, for your viewing pleasure, I present to you… What's your name, son?"

"Fuck you!"

"Mister Fuk Yu. Must be of Asian heritage."

The crowd laughs, raising their glasses in toast.

"Tonight's theme, as suggested by the ravishing Ms. Corva—good evening, madame—will be eminent German author Franz Kafka!"

The audience nods.

"In 1915, Kafka had published his seminal modernist work *Die Verwandlung*, aka 'The Metamorphosis', about a man's transformation into an insect. What better inspiration could we have for our production here, yes?"

His audience agrees.

Mister Holland again consults the cabinet, rubbing his chin while scanning the contents of the open drawer.

"Hmmm. Where shall we begin?"

With an air of theatricality, he snaps on a pair of latex gloves. He then lifts from the drawer a handheld pneumatic riveter.

Mister Holland looms over Steve, squirming in his restraints.

"I'll kill ya, you crazy fuck!"

Holland stoops to whisper into his ear. "Clear your mind of everything but the pain. Concentrate on the pain. Experience it. Express it. Let your pain *speak* for you." A broad smile stretches across his face. "Now let's give 'em their money's worth."

Mister Holland steps away, returning moments later wheeling in a large steel cart set with a variety of strange golden accoutrements. He parks it beside Steve.

"Please. Whatever you're doing... don't..."

"You're gonna be fine, son. Even better than that. I'm making you into a work of art."

From the cart Mister Holland picks up a near perfect replica of a bug's leg. Near perfect except for its size—must be four feet long. Steve thinks it the freakiest thing he has ever seen.

Holland raises the object for the audience to behold.

"I shall begin with the midlegs, modeled aptly enough after *Blattella germanica*, the German cockroach. These will not be functional as the replacement limbs will be, but here at *FYVP* we never skimp on authenticity."

Holland places the flattened upmost segment of the leg against Steve's flesh, between his fifth and sixth ribs... "No. Stop. *Please!*"...and with the riveter fastens the piece onto Steve's body.

Steve's pain screams for him.

The audience applauds wildly, as they do when the next leg is attached to the opposite side of Steve's torso.

Tears stream down Steve's face, the unbearable agony beyond anything he has known before. He begs for mercy, but even he can't make out his own words now.

Mister Holland pats him on the head. "Great show, son! We're killing 'em."

From the cabinet drawer Holland produces a rock hammer and chisel.

Steve's eyes widen in terror.

"Now, let's give you a proper mandible," Holland chimes and begins to chip away at Steve's jaw...

THE DARK AT THE DEEP END

"Nothing quite encourages as does one's first unpunished crime."

—Marquis de Sade,
from *The 120 Days of Sodom*

We lived near the water. The ocean had always been part of us. The smell of brine in the air. Nautical arts and crafts in every store, even Sal's Pizzeria. Plentiful seafood, seagulls. The sand in our clothes that never seemed to completely shake or wash out. Year round we would go to the beach. It took twenty minutes to reach by bike, less than five by car. It was most crowded in the summer, of course. People love to swim and play in the water. Not me. I would only go in if it was really hot out, and I'd never go out too far. Up to my waist, maybe my chest, my feet always touching the bottom. I was afraid of man-eating sharks and giant squids and fearsome creatures of the deep yet undiscovered.

People disappeared in the ocean, so I stayed close to shore. The land was safer. I knew my land—its roads, its neighborhoods, its Dunkin' Donuts and 7-Elevens and 24-hour diners.

I could hide here.

———

I didn't know what Brad had against Steve Higgleman. I'd heard they had some sort of altercation in the locker room during gym class, but I wasn't present for that and Brad told me nothing about what had happened. He was obviously mad about it. He wanted payback.

Three weeks later—you always waited a while before you carried out a revenge mission—we visited Capt. Bob's Fish Market on the canal. With our part-time job money we bought twenty mackerel and a few porgies. These were the cheapest and would serve our purpose just fine. Hours later, after 2 a.m., we struck.

We snuck into Higgleman's neighbor's yard. There were some tall hedges dividing the two properties. Brad had previously scoped out Higgleman's house, that's how he found out they had an inground pool in their yard. But we couldn't see it in the dark from behind those hedges. I could smell the fish we had, going bad. I wanted to get this over with.

Brad directed us to where we should position ourselves. Then we opened our plastic Capt. Bob's bags and, fish by fish, blindly catapulted them over the shrubs. Some we heard splash into the pool, our target. Others we heard thud against the cement and lawn. A couple smacked the metal slide, which made more of a racket than we'd wanted. My blood was pounding through my veins.

Twenty mackerels and six porgies had been too many!, I thought.

Then there were none left. We ran like idiots back to my car, our arms, our clothes, Jon's face, my Jesusy hair spattered with rotting fish guts. I put 7-Eleven bags over my hands so I didn't mess my steering wheel. My Toyota tore through the night. We gagged, laughed, and retched the whole way to my house. We hosed off in my yard. We still stank the next day, even after we'd each gone home and showered.

And that was how Brad rained justice down on Steve Higgleman.

The things we do for friends.

The second floor of Brad's house had two bedrooms. In one was his sister Tricia, thirteen years old, cute but kind of bubble-brained. The other bedroom belonged to his devout Catholic mom and his stepfather. Brad never called him that. It was either "my mom's boyfriend" or "Marty." Brad lived in the basement, as far as he could get from them while living under the same roof. He liked to draw comics and cartoons. All he did when he was home was sleep and draw. (The sketches appearing throughout these pages are some of his I've kept.)

Jon lived up the block from Brad. His father was an electrician and a mean drunk. Not violent mean, just angry mean. He'd yell and break things, which I suppose one could say *was* violent. But he never hit Jon or his little brother or his mom. Sometimes, when I picked Jon up, I could hear his dad thundering inside, rattling the windows. Jon didn't talk about him very much. Talked about his dad's boat way more than about him.

My parents were normal. They had brought me up normal. They encouraged my writing, even though I wasn't very good back then. Wrote the usual pretentious angsty shit teens write. By the time I started high school, my two older brothers were gone, one somewhere in Europe, the other dead. So it was just me, my mom and my dad. They didn't mind if I stayed out late, sometimes up until dawn. They were cool like that.

Brad, Jon, and I had met in junior high and we remained friends into high school even though we were in all different classes. I took mostly AP ones, while both Brad and Jon were dumped in with the remedial kids, though I think only Jon had some sort of actual learning disability. We'd gravitated toward each other because we didn't fit in anywhere else. We weren't jocks, or nerds, or art fags, or band geeks, or drama freaks. We never hung out at school. We'd always meet up by the theater after the last bell rang then hop into my car, a shamrock green 1982 Corolla that we dubbed the Deathmonger for no better reason than it sounded badass.

We would drive somewhere, nowhere, wherever, in search of something to do. That was our routine. That was our life. Formative years, they call these. And indeed I was formed—forged, really—into what I am today.

My appetite for mischief introduced itself in elementary school. I'd enjoyed getting blamed for offenses I had not committed. If a pencil or hat or blackboard eraser went missing, and the teacher asked the class if anybody knew where the item was, I pretended to harbor this knowledge by looking culpable, staring down at my desk and fidgeting my legs. The teacher would then ask me if I had taken the item. My eyes still averted, I shook my head. Sometimes she would inspect my desk or knapsack, of course finding nothing. I could tell she still did not believe me, but she couldn't prove my guilt. She was powerless to do anything. This excited me.

By fourth grade they put me on Ritalin.

Boys will be boys, they say. Some of the girls I had known back then were like boys too. We relentlessly sought out ways to amuse ourselves. Some days our gang would crouch on opposite sides of a street, wait for a car to approach, then tug an imaginary rope across the road. The more vigilant drivers would brake hard and glare at us. A few even got out to check if we were stretching something, maybe some sort of metal-shearing cable that could slice their car in half. We'd just stand there, looking innocent. Looking at them like they were stupid.

Me and my childhood friends Larry and Greg—the Verdusky twins—on one especially inspired afternoon at their house, were browsing the *Lost Pets* classifieds in the local paper. We settled on an ad labeled HEARTBROKEN. Dialed its number.

"Hello," an old-sounding woman answered.

"Hi," I said. "Did you lose a little white dog with a sparkly green collar? Name on the tag says Binky." I read this off the description in the ad.

"Yes we did! Did you find her?"

"Yep! On Grenada Ave, near the Foodtown."

"That's wonderful! The kids will be so happy!"

"Super. Is there a reward?"

"Yes there is! $50."

I lowered my voice an octave. "We want $300."

"$300! That's too much."

"Do you want Binky back or not?"

"Of course! But I can only give you $50."

"That's not enough."

"That's all you're getting, young man!"

"Then my buddies are just gonna keep kicking the crap out of your mutt until you pay up." Larry and Greg kicked a cardboard box and made whimpering noises in the background for effect.

"Stop it!" the old lady cried. "You awful—"

"We'll call you back. Give you time to think about how much Binky is worth to you and the kids."

Then I hung up. We never called back, of course.

It would've been a perfect prank, except for one lapse in planning: we had called our mark collect. When she received her phone bill, the Verdusky's home number was listed with the reverse charge info. It didn't take long for the old lady to contact the authorities, who pulled up the twins' address and sent two policemen there. Their mom answered the door. Once assured there was no little white dog with a sparkly green collar on the premises, the officers left. Larry and Greg both got grounded for a month.

I got in no trouble at all.

The Christmas season brought out our naughty sides in full force.

Jon owned a high-powered BB gun, an air rifle that took two CO2 tanks. It had impressive range, and Jon had good aim. For most of the year we tooled around town and shot out street lamps and car tires. During the holidays, we set our sights on the most irresistible prey: inflatable Xmas decorations. Soft-skinned Santas and reindeer, Frostys and candy canes, drunkenly swaying. They were not built to endure. They were not long for this world.

We'd cruise up to a house displaying one or more of these bloated abominations. Then Jon would lean out the rear window—I always drove, Brad always rode shotgun, and Big Jon had the entire backseat to himself, where he fired off a rapid succession of death-dealing steel pellets. The results were not immediate. We'd speed away, grab a bite at the 7-Eleven, then return to the scene of the slaying about an hour later.

How ever so gratifying it was to behold our victims, now mostly flaccid, with parts of them clinging to life, a mittened hand still raised, an antler still extended, their smiles transformed into crazed grins with the realization that, come morning, they'd likely wind up in the trash can, not worth the effort to patch up, no matter how much li'l

Sara or Davy begged their parents to save them. Mommy and Daddy would just buy a new pump-up Rudolph, until the high mortality rate convinced them to go with a hard shell model instead.

In a more ambitious, more thought-out scheme, we snatched from people's properties an assortment of the most distinctive holiday ornaments—one-of-a-kind home-made ones were especially coveted—storing them in my backyard shed until the next December when we would return them… to their *neighbor's* front lawns. We imagined we'd started scores of family feuds. While our imaginations were fertile, after a couple of years we grew dissatisfied we had never actually witnessed any of the outcomes. Did hot-tempered Mr. Harrison beat up Mr. Greeves over the theft of his hand-painted Santa's Village wall tarp? Did bully Billy Pulaski take a bat to Mrs. Wegman for swiping his animatronic gingerbread man? We never found out.

That was no fun.

As part of our annual heists, we abducted black Wise Men from outdoor Nativity scenes (including ones from the Bethport firehouse and the Hooksville train station). It wasn't a racial preference; rather, the black ones were typically the tallest of the three figures and they looked the sharpest in their regal robes. We accumulated almost a dozen over three years, all of which I kept in my shed. When my parents asked me where they had come from, I answered we salvaged them from people's trash. Mom and Dad bought my explanation. Or maybe they just did not want to upset me. I wasn't very nice when I was upset. Sometimes they wouldn't sleep until I cooled off.

I was thirteen when my brother Pete died in a car accident, totaling his restored '67 Mustang and himself. He had been drinking and driving, discovering he couldn't do both at the same time. He'd been a good brother, with a kind heart. The kind of heart that could not withstand colliding head-on with a concrete mixer. A tragedy, by all accounts.

All through the viewing at the funeral home, I remember my mother did not say a word. I guess she was still in shock, sitting in an armchair against the wall, only nodding at family and friends expressing their condolences. She wouldn't even look at her second-born son lying there in the open casket.

I couldn't take my eyes off Pete.

He was wearing my tie.

"It's OK," dad said when I pointed it out. "Pete looks good in it, doesn't he?"

But it wasn't OK. It was my favorite tie, a retro design of psychedelic amoeba shapes dancing in an alien sea. Mom bought it for me at the Fortunoff's in the mall. I wore it to most special occasions.

I told my dad I wanted it back.

"You can't have it," dad said.

"It's mine," I said.

He promised he'd buy me a new one.

I demanded it back.

"Please don't make a scene," dad said. "Not here."

I saw people were gawking at us.

"Nobody asked me," I grumbled and stomped out to the lobby, taking a seat in a big leather chair. I spent the remainder of the affair digging furrows into the chair's arms with my fingernails.

The next day, after Pete was buried, I came home to find the tie draped over my pillow. Dad must've asked the funeral director to replace it. I rolled it up and stuck it in my drawer with my other ties. I never wore that one again. Pretty much forgot about it.

Pete was the second real-life dead body I'd ever seen. The first I saw the year before while walking to school. I was taking a shortcut through the woods between my house and the junior high. As I crossed the creek I spotted a person sitting on the eroded bank, beneath a canopy of exposed tree roots.

It was this young scrawny guy, probably in his early twenties, in sandals, jeans, and a Pink Floyd T-shirt, with messy brown hair and a stubbly pale face. He slouched forward, holding a silver pistol limply in his lap. Lots of blood trailed out of his mouth and down his chin. There was a gaping hole in the back of his head—an exit wound. Obviously a suicide.

I understand why he chose this place to do it. It was peaceful and pretty secluded, but there were enough people who hiked and hung around there so eventually he would be found. His family and friends would know what had happened to him, which I suppose was better for them. For closure, I guess.

I picked up this long straight stick and poked at the hole in his head a bit. Then I stuck it in, slid it all the way through and out his slacking jaw a few inches. There were a few leaves sprouting from the other end of the stick. It looked like a small tree growing from his skull.

I left him there like that. Something to mystify his surviving loved ones. The stuff memories are made of.

The novelty of stowing an inanimate army of swarthy Wise Men eventually ebbed. One night, we loaded them all up in my car—three in the trunk, six in the backseat with Jon, two in Brad's lap—and drove to the end of the canal. There we filled each with enough seashell gravel to weigh them down, then heaved them into the water, which swallowed them whole.

Afterward I dropped the guys off. We got to Brad's house first, close to 3 a.m. The light in his parents' bedroom was off, while his sister's was on. "Tricia's up," Jon said. I knew he had a crush on her, but she was jailbait. And she didn't like boys.

Brad stiffened, as he always did when he came home to the same situation. And I could feel from him that it *was* a situation, though he never shared with Jon and me what bothered him. Only once did I ask him what was wrong. Nothing, he answered, which meant that it was none of my business. At the time, I was kind of pissed by this. Friends confided in each other, it was a barometer of trust. Now I can admit I was just being nosy. We didn't tell each other *everything*. Some things we bury inside us, digging them up when the mood compels us, and then shovel the dirt right back over them.

Without a word Brad exited my car and crept into his house. I wanted to honk my horn, wake everybody in his family up, see what happened, but I didn't.

The living room light in Jon's house was turned on when we pulled up. I knew that meant his dad was awake and wasted, so Jon didn't go in. He said he was going for a walk. Like usual, he did not want to hang out more. We seldom hung out without Brad. It felt weird doing it, like we were missing an essential circuit that kept us running properly. Jon put on his headphones and started hiking down the block. I went home.

That night, and many nights after, I dreamt all the plastic Magi, glowing ethereally, had surrounded my bed, regarding me with their luminous dead eyes. "*Why are you here?*" I screamed, and bubbles spilled from my mouth—they hadn't come to me, I'd been taken to them, under the water. Yet I wasn't scared. Here I was a god.

The dockside spot where we'd sunk them was about five feet deep. In the daylight you could see them through the murk, clustered on the canal bed. Over the next few months I had gone back several times. Their paint peeled off, replaced by mottles of algae and barnacles. Schools of minnows zipped about them, nibbling from their husks. Soon marine life and litter had concealed them entirely, and now only I remember they're down there. That's how I want it. That's how some things need to be.

———⋙⋘———

During Easter break of our junior year, Jon's cousin Randy visited from Connecticut. He was one of those martial arts buffs, always wearing this shiny black jacket with patches all over it featuring dragons and cobras and Oriental words. We were never sure if he really practiced karate, tae kwon do, or jiu-jitsu like he claimed. He'd show us some fancy moves, but for all we knew he could've copied them from kung fu movies. He never brought over the belts he supposedly earned. Always forgot. Always promised he would next time.

What he always did bring was any new weaponry he had collected. On prior occasions, it was Asian stuff he'd picked up at tradeshows: nunchucks, throwing stars, butterfly knives, and an awesome Samurai sword with a phoenix etched into its blade.

This time, though, he brought something different, something better—a compound bow. It was charcoal gray, with pulleys on each end. Randy told us the bow was made of aircraft-grade aluminum, with steel strings.

We wanted to see it in action. Randy was happy to oblige us. We trekked into the woods beyond the railroad tracks where many of the kids from our school partied at night. As we'd hoped, nobody was there because it was too early, still daylight. We set up a bunch of empty beer cans on a decaying log and took turns trying to hit them with silver-tipped arrows. It was like a carnival game. Brad, Jon, and I sucked at it. To his credit, Randy was an ace shot. He missed only once, and that was because at the moment he released his arrow a deer bounded out of the brush. Randy missed that fucker too. We left when it got so dark out we could not see anything anymore. But we weren't ready to quit playing.

It was Brad who'd suggested going to Satan's house. Satan was actually Mr. Vincent, our vice principal. He had sentenced Brad to detention no less than a dozen times for tardiness. Brad, believing Mr. Vincent had it out for him, retaliated by drawing pictures of his nemesis with devil horns and fiendish fangs. Sometimes he replaced Vincent's pornstache with snakes. I have to say, the pictures of him weren't unflattering likenesses. Many of them had a wicked appeal.

Mr. Vincent's address was listed in the phone book. We drove there after midnight, after watching the movie *Dreamscape* which Jon had rented from the video store. We parked across the street a few houses down. There were no lights on in Satan's house. We approached stealthily and stood in the moon-flecked shadows of a maple tree. Randy raised his bow, aimed, and fired an arrow through the front door. It hardly made a sound, just a dull thunk like a paper punch. We ran like hell back to my car. Made a clean getaway.

It wasn't until the following week that we learned the arrow had killed Mr. Vincent's dog. It must've been lying by the door, or was passing by it at the instant of impact. I wondered what kind of dog it had been, hoping it was a cocker spaniel or a poodle. I wondered what it was like to wake up to find your pet skewered. It must've upset Mr. Vincent. He didn't show up at school for the rest of that week.

It also really upset Jon. Owning a dog himself—this slobbery golden retriever named Carly—he'd developed a soft spot for animals. Guess he blamed Brad and me for what happened to Satan's pooch, which was stupid since Randy was *his* cousin. At any rate, Jon didn't hang out with us for almost three months. He wouldn't answer his phone when we called or come to the door when we dropped by. He was being lame.

Sometimes we'd spot him walking around the neighborhood listening to his Discman. We'd pull up beside him and urge him to rejoin us. We reminded Jon that we didn't mean to whack the dog, that it wasn't even Jon's dog, that Mr. Vincent had once yanked Jon out of the cafeteria by the collar (for adding red food dye to all the toilets) while everyone laughed at him. At first, Jon simply ignored our logic and pleas. Later we knew we were wearing him down when he told us to "Fuck off!" Finally, at the end of June, we reminded him July 4th was near. We had always spent the holiday together. To this he yielded, reoccupying his place in the backseat of the Deathmonger.

We then returned to our regularly scheduled programming.

Fourth of July Eve tradition decreed Jon help himself to a bounty of his dad's re-stocked stash of fireworks. He grabbed roman candles and sky rockets, mortar shells and wheels, fountains and spinners. Then, in the dead of night, we prowled the sleeping towns in search of our prey.

I'd roll up alongside a parked car or van. Brad would get out and recon the area for any spying neighbors before checking the vehicle's doors. If it was unlocked, he'd give us the thumbs-up and dash back to my car. Meanwhile, Jon would jump out, light one or two pieces of artillery, and toss them into the chosen vehicle. Upon his return, I would take us to the end of the block, pausing there so we could witness our handiwork.

The fireworks ignited gloriously inside our marks, producing a bottled spectacle of rainbow-colored crosettes and chrysanthemums, palms and peonies, stars and strobes. Within seconds, the smoke and flames would overwhelm the magnificent pyrotechnicalia, our cue to flee.

The final time we'd pulled this off, we lit up a dozen vehicles across five towns. The last car nearly proved our undoing. After we sparked a Catherine wheel in a Cadillac, we rode up the street, where we were greeted head-on by a police cruiser. I just kept driving past him acting all calm and casual, though I was shitting my pants. I turned round the corner and as soon as the pig was out of sight I punched the gas. We sped through a maze of side streets away from the scene, then navigated our way to the turnpike. We went home and hoped we had not become wanted men.

The following days I'd anxiously scanned the local paper and watched the TV news. Plenty of stories about robberies, house fires, and domestic violence, but nothing about our wave of vehicular vandalism.

We had gotten away with it.

———————×———————

The Verdusky twins died at home together at age 17.

Since our bygone days of crank calling—we lost touch after we started going to different junior high schools—the brothers had established quite the reputation for themselves and their wayward behavior. They had racked up a sundry criminal record, charged with multiple counts of indecent exposure, grand theft auto, grave desecration, etc.

Their preferred activity by far was setting fires to anything that could catch fire. They began with the wooded areas beside the parkway. They then moved up to the contents of mailboxes and dumpsters. One time, at the Sacred Shores Church, they burned several hymnals in a pile on the altar, and one of them climbed up the king-sized crucifix and charred Christ's nose with a lighter. Ultimately, they torched their own bedroom, with them still in it, and perished in the blaze.

Everyone thought their fate suited them. Everyone seemed glad they were gone.

I felt a little sorry for Larry and Greg. They couldn't control themselves. They were clearly sick, at the whim of their mental defects. For them, it wasn't about having fun. Their deeds were compulsive, an addiction. I wondered if they knew this and had sacrificed themselves to be free of the demons in their DNA. Maybe they realized they could never deny their degenerate natures, that they would never have a choice.

Me, I can stop myself anytime I want.

———————

It was our final night of summer vacation before we began our senior year. We puttered around the nearly deserted roads in the Deathmonger, stereo blaring Skynyrd's "Free Bird" while we yakked about the cool movies we saw, the bitchy teachers and snotty girls and dumb jocks we knew. People who needed to be reckoned with. We'd made a list.

Jon, wearing his snug Charles Manson T-shirt, announced he was hungry. I was a little hungry too. I spotted the 24-hour Dunkin' Donuts nestled in a strip mall between a dry cleaners and a drug store. I pulled into the lot and parked in front of the shop.

We shuffled in, my cowboy boots resounding off the tiles. A plump, grizzled hostess, coffee-stained apron tied about her waist, stood behind the counter, wiping it down with a damp washcloth.

"Good evening, boys," she welcomed us.

Brad plunked himself in the nearest booth while Jon and me ambled up to the cash register. Jon smiled at the gallery of pastries, then stopped smiling when the hostess thought he was smiling at her. I ordered a plain cruller and a milk. Jon got a cinnamon roll, warmed, with butter. Brad didn't want anything.

There were only two other customers in the shop.

An old, scraggly man in a rumpled beige sports coat sat alone at the rearmost booth, staring straight ahead at the opposite wall. He chatted aloud with an invisible companion as he sipped a cup of black coffee, a stubby unlit cigar pinched between his fingertips.

A youngish woman with strawy hair, yellowed teeth, and big boobs was perched on a stool at the counter, the paleness of her skin and the scabs on her face accentuated by the fluorescent lighting. Hands trembling, she chewed on her fingernails, glancing all around her, nervous, suspicious. Her foot tapped the floor to an imagined beat.

Jon and I joined Brad at the table and started eating our food. The shop door swung open. Two cops entered and approached the hostess. She discreetly pointed out the twitchy woman. The officers, both solemn and imposing, advanced upon her.

"Excuse me," one cop said.

She did not react.

"Are you feeling alright, miss?"

She stared down at the countertop, then at the clock on the wall, then out the window. Eyes darting everywhere but on the stern figures towering over her.

The other cop—Bad Cop—spoke more authoritative. "You'll have to leave now. You can't stay here all night."

"We're sorry, miss," Good Cop added.

No response.

"We can cite you for loitering, you know that?"

"C'mon, miss. Please." Good Cop gestured for her to get up and go.

The woman let out an exasperated sigh, clenching her fists. "Fuckin' bullshit," she spat, scowling. She mumbled something else at them as she sprang from the stool and stormed from the shop. Only then did I notice she was not wearing any shoes. The bottoms of her feet were dirty, almost black.

The hostess thanked the officers. They both requested large coffees, and Bad Cop asked for a cheese danish. The geezer in the back remained absorbed in his fantasy conversation.

Finishing our meals, we exited swiftly, avoiding the scrutiny of the snacking, slacking lawmen. As we got into my car, Jon saw the woman hoofing down the turnpike.

"Let's follow her," proposed Brad.

I nodded. Jon laughed.

It was something to do.

———— ✦ ————

None of us possessed much skill with the opposing sex. Brad largely acted disinterested, maybe because they confused or intimidated him. And Jon was not handsome or hunky enough to attract the kind of girls he was attracted to. I told him he should lower his standards, but he liked what he liked. I couldn't fault him for that.

I was, in comparison, luckiest with the ladies. Every few months I'd manage to score a date. And I scored poorly. They were generally one-off affairs, each typified by a combination of banal conversation, awkward silences, and drifting eyes.

Once, though, I'd experienced a fantastic night out with a girl named Jessica. I met her at a record store where she worked as a sales clerk. She dug the music I was buying, and I dug her strawberry blonde hair and jade green eyes. She gave me her number. I called her the next day and we made plans to get together that weekend.

I picked her up Saturday night and took her to one of the nicer Greek diners in the county. I bought her dinner, moussaka casserole, while I ordered the stuffed flounder. We talked and laughed with ease. Afterward, we went to the canal where I got us both Italian ices. We ate them at Capt. Bob's Fish Market while goggling at the live crabs and eels. Lastly we hit the arcade. I gave her five dollars in quarters for the machines. For most of our two hours there we played games against one another, side by side, her arm sometimes around my waist.

Best first date I've ever had.

On the ride back to her house, she became deathly quiet, hardly saying a word at all no matter how much I wheedled her. Upon dropping her off, she confessed she still had feelings for her ex. She couldn't be with me until she figured out things with him. She told me she was sorry, she had a great time, she'd call me if her and Aaron were definitely over. We said goodbye and that was that.

I'd spent $23.85 on her and I didn't even get a kiss.

Years later I found her again.

This time I made her pay.

The barefooted woman had wandered onto a branching road of duplex apartment houses, walking on the right side sidewalk. I caught up, coasting my car alongside her, and honked the horn twice. She didn't, or wouldn't, acknowledge our presence.

I judged she was about thirty, maybe younger, maybe older. She carried no bags or purse, was dressed in a pink tank top and blue jeans with a gaping tear up the thigh. Tiny beads of sweat clung to her brow.

Brad rolled down his window. "Need a lift, lady?"

The woman's pace quickened.

"Hey," I then blurted, leaning over Brad's shoulder. "Those cops had no right chasing you out of there. It's a public place."

"Yeah," Brad played along. "You weren't doing anything wrong."

Our feigned support worked to win her wary trust. She halted.

"They always do that," she said, scratching the bridge of her nose. "It's 'cause those sonsuvabitches don't like me 'round if I don't buy shit from 'em."

"Cops hassle you a lot, huh?" Brad asked.

"I'm fuckin' broke. I don't even know where the hell I am. What town is this?"

"East Milford," Brad answered.

She didn't seem to recognize the name.

"Any of you got a cigarette?"

None of us smoked.

"We're on our way to get gas," I said. "You can come with us and get cigs there, if you want."

She was visibly reluctant, teetering from one foot to the other.

"Where are you off to?" Brad asked.

"I'm tryin' to find the Department of Social Services."

"Why?"

"I'm lookin' for a job. Heard they can help me."

I offered to take her there, despite none of us having a clue where the Department of Social Services was located.

To my surprise, the woman was willing. She hopped into the backseat next to Jon. The stench she brought in with her was incredible, a b.o. bomb of near nuclear proportions. It must've been even worse for Jon. He slid away from her as far as possible, positioning himself so the wind from his open window would blow in his face.

We stopped at the Mobil gas station to fill up. Brad purchased from the Pakistani attendant a pack of menthols for the woman, no doubt a manipulative token of generosity. Without thanking him, she eagerly popped a cigarette from the box and stuck it between her quivering lips. She touched the tip with a match. Took a deep, desperate drag off it.

I volunteered to dial 411 to get the address for the Department of Social Services. She pleaded for me not to bother. I tried reassuring her, insisting it would only take a minute.

"Probably thinks you're gonna call the cops on her," Brad whispered into my ear.

"I'm just calling Information," I told her. "That's all. I promise."

I ran over to the pay phone by the gas station garage.

While they waited for me, I could see the woman shaking and sucking on her cigarette, and Jon breathing through his wide-open mouth, his entire face jutting out the window. A minute later I returned to the car.

"It's on Whaleneck Avenue," I said as I shifted into gear. "In Elkhurst."

Elkhurst was only about ten minutes away using the expressway, but I chose an indirect route with lots of traffic signals so Brad and I could get better acquainted with our passenger.

"Where're you from?" asked Brad.

"Brooklyn," she replied. "But I don't live there anymore."

"Where are you living now?"

"Nowhere," she murmured.

"What happened?"

"This rich guy, some kind of lawyer, was lettin' me stay with him."

"Was he your boyfriend?"

"No. Not really."

"Did he kick you out?"

"I left him… uhm… 'bout a week ago."

"Why'd you leave?"

"He drank a lot," she croaked. "And he was rough, sometimes."

"He beat you?"

"Yeah. Sometimes."

"Did he abuse you sexually?" probed Brad nonchalantly, like he was simply asking her if she had ever gone camping or tried sushi.

I fantasized about fucking her. Us taking turns with her. Or all at once, each of us plugging a hole. I wondered if she would enjoy it, and thank us for loving her, however shallow and fleeting that love may be.

"Why d'ya wanna know that?" she snarled.

Brad shrugged. "Just curious, that's all."

Jon checked his watch, groaned, and prayed for god to help him.

"I don't wanna talk 'bout it," she said.

I wondered if we could hurt her. Sure, we could go all the way with her. She was obviously mentally ill, probably homeless and a drug addict. Nobody would notice if she vanished. Nobody would care.

Nobody.

…We take the woman to the abandoned paper mill, force her into the building. It is barren inside, a forgotten place. We gag her with an oily rag, tie her to a rusty beam with bungee cords, and strip her naked. Like her head hair, her pubes are a jungly mess. We sizzle them off with a bbq lighter, then roast her clit, burn her inner thighs, and bake her lips. With a hammer we knock out four of her teeth. With scissors we snip off her nipples and sever the fingers from both her hands. We pluck out one of her eyes using the clamp of a booster cable. We take turns lashing her ass with a car antenna until it bleeds, then pour gasoline into the gashes and light them up. We drive a hot screwdriver into her pussy, then into her ass. Next, we peel the flesh away from the bones of her arms and legs with a box cutter, then lay her nerves bare in three adjacent places, the nerve ends tied to a short stick which is twisted like a tourniquet, stretching the nerves taut, causing her to suffer unheard-of agony. We give her some rest, then continue working on her. With the screwdriver Brad bores a hole in her throat, draws her tongue back down through it, which looks funny as hell. Clutching the box cutter, I thrust my hand into her pussy and cut through the partition dividing the anus from the vagina. I toss aside the cutter, reinsert my hand, and rummage about her entrails, making her shit through her pussy, another amusing stunt. Next, we focus on her face: cut away her ears, burn her nasal passages, blind her remaining eye with broken glass, and scalp her. We split her belly open and apply a torch to her guts. Then Jon burrows into her chest with his pocketknife and punctures her heart in several places…

I pictured all this. But I never touched her. None of us did.

But we could have, and that excited me.

We reached the closed Social Services building at the third major intersection on Whaleneck Avenue. Next to it was a 24-hour White Castle. Their hamburgers were small, but were only 49¢ each and addictively delicious.

"Place won't be open until nine I guess," I told her. "I'm gonna let you off here, OK?"

I steered into the restaurant lot. Before I came to a complete stop the woman leapt from the car and beelined for the burger joint's entrance, slipping into the brightly lit sanctuary without giving us so much as a farewell flip-off. That's gratitude for you.

"She smelled sooo bad," Jon said. He recommended I disinfect my car.

I took Brad and Jon home and kept on driving, immersed in my thoughts, until it was time to go to school.

———◦✶◦———

Few months later, Brad almost beat his stepfather to death for molesting his sister, caving his head in with her flute case. Brad was sentenced to juvee for a year, then went to live with his real dad upstate. Not sure if he's still there. For the rest of our senior year, Jon and I didn't hang out much. It just wasn't the same without Brad. After graduating, Jon enrolled at a college in Colorado. He only comes back on holidays. I never do anything with him when he's in town.

I have to entertain myself these days.

Whenever I have a night off, I like going to the beach. Sitting on the sand, blending in with the darkness around me. It's comforting. I gaze out at the water, ghostly wisps of crashing surf appearing then disappearing on its otherwise inky surface.

I remember how I used to wonder what lay beneath it. But I didn't dare go in. I wasn't ready.

Not yet.

SUITABLE FOR FRAMING

I make my living aiming my lens on the human condition. What a shit show that usually is. And people want me to stick their noses in it. They crave their own stink.

It's masochistic.

I really can't complain though. I've earned a respectable income photographing things most folks turn away from. Seven years ago I'd established myself with my very first gallery exhibition titled *Hit and Run*, featuring visceral black-and-white images of roadkill in situ. Then came my breakout series, *Beautiful Smiles*, composed of wall-sized prints of broken teeth, cracked lips, and cleft palates. This was followed by three more acclaimed projects: *Stains & Blights*, *The Fall of Man* (pictures of neglected religious structures, recipient of the Kraszna-Krausz Book Award), and *Screaming Heads*.

All my work fetches premium prices. It still amazes me, just a little, that somebody would want a photo of a mangled possum on their foyer's wall, or of cum-crusted panties draped over an empty box of disposable diapers. But ugliness presented aesthetically has always been in demand. The Nazis used to make lampshades out of Jew skin. Today one of those—if you can even find the genuine article on the black market—would set you back a few hundred grand. There's always someone who will gladly pay it.

My new project I might call *Peeping*, but that sounds kind of sophomoric. Maybe *Peep Show*. That's provocative, if unoriginal.

At least I don't have to leave home for this one. The convenience is definitely a bonus. I don't have to shower, get dressed, brush my teeth. Working dirty suits me. And there's the additional benefit of not having to intermingle with any of those assholes and dumbshits out there. I can order everything I need online and get it delivered right here 24/7.

I live on the top floor of a luxury high-rise. It merits the label "luxury" for its prime location, state-of-the-art kitchen (though I don't cook), and a doorman who's paid handsomely to keep the tenants' private lives private. He always gets a generous Xmas tip from me.

The view leaves something to be desired. My window looks out on a tall wall of other windows belonging to the neighboring apartment tower. A mosaic of the mundane, if you are looking at it from the eyes of a tenant. But the artist's eye offers a much different perspective, as long as it's on duty. Aside from my darkroom, my home had been solely my place of relaxation and recreation, not of inspiration. And the more familiar you become with something, the more blinded you are to its possibilities, its potential.

And then one day, maybe, you see it.

———⋈———

The day I saw it I'd just returned from a crapshoot, which is when I go out photographing random stuff in hopes I hit pay dirt. This rarely occurs. The vast majority of the time the shots turn out to be discardable dreck. Often the subject ruins their candidness. When people spot a camera pointed at them, they either want to shun it, punch it, razz it, or fuck it. None of these work. The subjects should never have a relationship with the camera. It should be a god they cannot observe, have no knowledge of its existence. Otherwise it becomes just another bullshit religion.

I made prints of the day's worthless bounty and hung them on the stone mantel. From the sofa I took potshots at each with my air rifle, riddling them with holes until their banality was obliterated.

This was only mildly satisfying.

While I sat there in my boxers idly stroking my gun and staring out the window, I noticed something I hadn't before. Aquariums. That's what the wall of windows of the apartment building opposite mine resembled. Thirty-two huge fish tanks stacked one on top of another in rows of four. In each people swam in their private worlds, seemingly unaware they could be watched, scrutinized, judged.

In one tank, this anorexic girl in a leotard bounced around to an exercise show on TV. Two floors up, a Latino (or Arab) dude wearing a baby blue blazer was giving tango lessons to a fat lady in a floral sundress. Diagonally to the left, a family of five ate supper at a round table, mother yelling at her two pajamaed kids while father fed soup to their ancient grandmother.

People are never more true, less on guard, than when they are inside their own homes. Sure, most of the time it's just the same old, same old. Lives unadorned and uninteresting. But odds are, afloat in their sweet obliviousness, there will be a delicious moment they display their primal, perverse, pitiful tendencies. All I had to do was wait for it. Not such an unappealing prospect in the comfort of my own home.

After switching off all the lights in my apartment, I hauled out my trusty Leica DSLR camera with 80-400mm telephoto lens and mounted it on my Sachtler fluid tripod, a holdover from my days shooting 35mm. I set the rig in front of my window, sparked a cig, and hunted for treasure within those glass and steel containers.

That first night I snapped about a hundred pics and had panned only a single gold nugget: an underwear-clad, beer-bellied guy lazing in a wide leather recliner, his white T-shirt stained with vomit. He was alone, and had been all night, a conical birthday hat strapped to his head.

A 1% return on my time investment. It was enough.

In the morning I called my agent Chas Grubstein and told him about my concept.

"Hallefuckinlujah," he said.

We then discussed the legalities of invading people's privacy in the name of art. I suggested we blur out anything that could identify the subject, maybe Photoshop smiley faces on everybody. Grubs thought this was a terrific idea. It'll be the official follow-up to *Beautiful Smiles*, he said. Not really, I thought, but what the hell. He was excited. I like it when my agent is excited. He's much less whiny.

"St. Martin's wants to see something in three weeks. At least half of it."

"I bet," I boasted, "I have the whole goddamned book for 'em."

———————————

That was three months ago.

I caught a naked bodybuilder shooting dope on his weight bench. This little boy in an army soldier costume spanking his napping mother. A middle-aged guy with no kids fixing the broken tail on a toy dinosaur. A teen girl in a torn prom dress crying in front of her mirror. A three-legged Siamese cat sunning itself beside an empty bottle of JD. I have maybe a dozen decent shots that'll probably make the cut.

It's not enough.

My agent is riding my ass hard, of course. I tell him I can't predict instances of indelible reality. Grubs tells me St. Martin's is threatening to drop my contract. I scoff. He whines. It's making me anxious, and an anxious artist produces slapdash work, hack grade shit. Fuck that. I got my integrity to consider. My reputation. My fans. Great artists don't settle for mediocrity just to earn a paycheck. I would rather starve.

Fortunately, Saturday night serves me up a feast.

Together, his chest glued to her back, they shuffle into the 8th floor corner apartment. They're one of those young and attractive hipster couples, smartly dressed and dumbly drunk. I knew it was the chick's place, so the guy has to be her hot date du jour. Many of her dates wound up at her place, in her bed. I'd captured her carnal trysts no less than six times before. The first occasion was pretty titillating. Now it's like watching an old porn video you've seen so often you could hum along with all the music. On the way from the front door to her bedroom, they shuck off their clothes like rusting robots.

The woman is gorgeous. Blonde, slim, long legs, big tits. Nothing special. The man is soap star handsome, yawn inducing. He shuts the bedroom door behind them, spins the woman around by her waist, and kisses her with well-honed passion. It may as well have been choreographed. He clumsily guides her to the canopy bed. They collapse onto it, probing and groping one another in all of the expected spots. They ultimately arrange themselves into the standard missionary position. I take a few perfunctory pics, but I'm not harboring any delusions of snapping anything remarkable. And then something extraordinary happens.

His pelvis pounds into hers, harder, faster, and I anticipate the usual climax. But next he wraps his huge hands around her slender throat. She initially appears to enjoy his fire, his ferocity, until she realizes the grievousness of his intentions. She latches onto his forearms, trying to tear his paws away from her neck, digging her fingernails into his flesh. He squeezes tighter. She chokes, he cums.

She dies.

I freeze, but only for an instant. A professional artist cannot afford to squander moments like these. I continue clicking.

The man releases his grip. I see his hands have left a deep red imprint on her milky skin. Her mouth and eyes gape. He stares at her, what's left of her. He runs his finger-tips across her lips. He then dismounts and sits on the edge of the bed, his sweat-glistened back to her. He appears both peaceful and panicked, the extremes of his experience, the gratification and the gravity of it, colliding and converging within him.

He peers out the window—right at me—then looks away. He cannot see me in my shadows.

The man rises from the bed, gathers his clothes, and hastily dresses himself. He scans the apartment, probably for anything that might be incriminating. However much he cleans up after himself, I'm sure it will not be nearly enough. Dude must've dropped more DNA there to convict him for multiple lifetimes. But he does what he can and skedaddles.

I wonder about him. I wonder if he has done this before, if all his dates end this way, if he'd killed kittens as a kid. I wonder until I stop caring. He doesn't matter anymore. I can no longer observe him through my lens.

I direct my attentions toward her. I had not only witnessed her final breaths and bucks but recorded them. My photos alone can seal her paramour's fate. Aside from the evidential value, I consider their artistic merit. I should be thrilled, but I'm not. What did I really capture? Another crime of passion. Another one-day news headline. Murder is so ordinary, so routine. So uninspired.

I decide nobody will ever see the photos. They were not even interesting enough to jack off to.

I focus in on her body, her corpse. Her shell. I take a single shot, a close-up of her face. She is still beautiful. Typical beautiful. Too beautiful.

My fans crave more.

The doorman lets me through. He knows me. My Spanish friend Hector, an illustrator, lives there on the 5th floor. We sometimes do blow together on his glasstop billiards table.

I'm not concerned about being accused of the crime. There will be no trace of my presence at the scene. I am wearing these stylish leather driving gloves and a woolen cap. I take the elevator up to the 5th floor, then the stairs to the 8th. It's quiet. Like my building, there are no surveillance cameras in the hallways or stairwells. Her date had left her door unlocked, as I'd hoped, so I have no trouble accessing her apartment.

Upon entering, I promptly draw all the blinds. Her bedroom smells like booze, sex, and perfume. She looks like she's sleeping. She's definitely not breathing though. I made certain of it.

I survey the room. In a rattan chair is sprawled one of those Harlequin clown puppets with a porcelain face. I grab it and start a pile. I find her fuzzy raccoon slippers and her cosmetic box, with enough shades and shadows for eyes, cheeks, and lips to make herself look like a thousand different versions of herself. In her nightstand she stows her vibrator and an assortment of condoms. I leave them there; these are too easy, too pedestrian. I move on. In the hallway closet I uncover a roll of purple ribbon, Christmas lights, a zebra-print scarf, a green umbrella, and a bicycle pump. From her desk I scoop up a stapler and a pair of scissors. From the den I collect a bronze Buddha statue and a potted cactus. From the bathroom, a can of shaving cream and a polka-dotted shower cap. I hit the kitchen next. From the fridge I pull out a jar of dill pickles, ketchup, mustard, mayo, a bunch of carrots, an apple, and some deli meats. From the drawers a corkscrew, cheese grater, lemon reamer, metal tongs, spoons, forks, and an expensive set of steak knives (I own the same ones).

Then I go to work on her.

I return to my place an hour later.

After finishing up at Sleeping Beauty's I'd roamed the city blocks in search of a cop car sans cops. I located one parked on 71st. The two officers were across the street inside a 7-Eleven, posted at the condiment station perfecting their supersized cups of coffee. On their windshield under the wipers I left the note I'd written on the back of a LOST DOG flyer.

HOMICIDE IN

WYDELL BUILDING

APT. 809

I only have to wait about twenty minutes. The cop car cruises up to Wydell's lobby entrance and the officers swagger in. Less than five minutes later the doorman lets them into her apartment. They switch on the lights, which I had turned off before I re-opened the blinds.

The officers, pistols ready, ease their way through the den. One veers off to check out the bathroom, the other the kitchen. They reunite at her bedroom door. They go in. Flip on the light. Gaze upon her.

There's a sublime moment as the scene sinks in when time seems to stop. Nobody moves. I click a pic.

The shorter officer hunches over and pukes on his glossy oxford shoes. His partner stands there slack-jawed, shocked. But wait… is that a hint of a grin playing on his lips? Maybe he's a fan.

Click. Click. Click. Click. Click.

Today I will have enough for my book. For my fans.

I'm giving them the quintessence of human aesthetic inverted: an object of beauty uglified for the masses.

Desecrated. Decimated. Transcended.

Yeah, let them take a good whiff of this shit. I know they'll love it.

Somebody always does.

EVERYONE
IS A MOON

ACKNOWLEDGEMENTS

I would like to express my appreciation and gratitude to:
Emily Russell, Russ Colchamiro, Heather Hutsell, Beckie
McDowell, Ali Mogar Hunt, St. Joseph's University Graduate
Writing Studies Program, West Philly Writers Group, and
my family and friends for all their feedback and support
over the years.

ABOUT THE AUTHOR

Sawney Hatton is an author, editor, and screenwriter who has long loved taking trips to the dark side.

Weaned on a steady diet of paranormal horror and creature features, he quickly developed an appetite for all things macabre and monstrous. With early literary influences as tonally disparate as Stephen King's *Pet Sematary*, Evelyn Waugh's *The Loved One*, and Marquis de Sade's *The 120 Days of Sodom*, he enjoys fusing the sinister with the satirical, the abominable with the absurd.

Other incarnations (reincarnations?) of Sawney have produced marketing videos, attended all-night film fests, and played the banjo and sousaphone (not at the same time).

As of this writing he is still very much alive.

Visit the author's website at
www.SawneyHatton.com

Manufactured by Amazon.ca
Acheson, AB

12735756R00116